Keg's Revelation

Haven MC
Book Three

by Carson Mackenzie

CM Books, LLC

Published by CM Books, LLC
Copyright © Oct 2019 Carson Mackenzie
Cover Design by Carson Mackenzie
Photographer: Paul Henry Serres
Cover Model: Mikaël Jodoin
ISBN# 978-1-952184-25-3

If you find any books being sold or shared illegally, please contact the author at carsonmackenzieauthor2020@gmail.com.

CM Books, LLC

Synopsis

Reed "Keg" Borelli loves his freedom, and to him, nothing beats hitting the open road with his club brothers. At least it used to be that way before two of them settled down with ol' ladies. He is happy for his brothers, maybe even a little jealous. Keg once thought he had found love. Instead, he chalked it up to being young.

Until she returns.

Raven Allen is back in the town she was raised in. Except for this time as a woman with responsibilities and harboring at least one regret. She figures life has come full circle when she faces the man who, at a young age, had held her whole heart. But if life had taught her anything – it was happiness wasn't meant for her. She experienced it twice, and each time it had been ripped away.

Haven MC is placed on standby when a local gang steps up their illegal activity. The situation isn't generally in the realm of their directives, but as the gang's activity threatens to touch one of their own – the sphere changes – and Keg realizes he can either hold on to the feeling of betrayal or grasp the second chance life has offered.

CM Books, LLC

Table of Contents

CM Books, LLC

CM Books, LLC

Prologue

Keg

The door bounced off the wall after I kicked it open. When I stepped through the doorway, it swung back in my direction, giving me a split second to catch it. Then I slammed it so hard the pictures on the adjoining wall rattled.

One of the best days had turned so fast. Riding the high of being patched from prospect to member—only to lose the high a few hours later when it came crashing and burning around me.

"Damn it, what the hell, Reed? Your ass is lucky I didn't step out of the office and shoot you. Thought some jackass was busting in," my dad said as he stopped halfway down the hallway of our house and lowered the nine-millimeter he currently held in his hand. "Weren't you headed to Raven's house?"

"I went," I said and walked past him toward the kitchen. It was the first free time I'd had off in a month. All I wanted was to sit with my girl on her front porch or maybe

9

take her for a ride on my bike to celebrate my patch-in. Ever since I started prospecting for the club, our time together consisted of a couple hours here and there when the club hadn't needed me. Now as a full member, I was looking forward to spending more time with her.

"Then why are you here trying to destroy the front door?" My dad stood in the doorway and watched as I opened the fridge and stared inside at its contents.

"Broke it off with her." A few seconds ticked by after my response. Slamming the door on the refrigerator, I yelled, "Shit!"

"Well, what happened? Because the last I heard before leaving the clubhouse was you telling the others, you wouldn't be celebrating with them. That you were going to celebrate with your girl." My dad's brow lifted, and he stared at me.

Leaning against the counter, rubbing my hand across the back of my neck, it felt as if I was coming out of my skin.

"That had been the plan, at least until I got there. Seems Raven's mom was in a car accident and was banged up pretty bad. Raven and her grandparents are leaving to be with her."

"Okay, she has a family emergency and is going out of town to help her mom. It's not as if you can't see her when she returns. That isn't a reason to—"

"The Newhouses will be back. Raven will be staying indefinitely," I said through clenched teeth, cutting my dad off and straightening from my position.

10

"What? I didn't think Raven got along with the stepdad, and that's why she chose to stay with her grandparents when her mom and he moved to the east coast."

"I brought that up when she said she didn't know if she'd be coming back. He travels a lot with his job, so she won't have to deal with him often. Raven's staying because her mom is going to need help long after she's allowed to go home from the hospital. The doctors don't know how long it will take her to get back to a hundred percent. That's if she even gets there. After they performed emergency surgery to stop internal bleeding and set her arm and leg that were broken, she had a stroke. Now she's having problems with her vision and speech, plus weakness on her right side."

"Damn, it must have been a helluva accident."

"Five cars and an eighteen-wheeler on the interstate. Her mom was one of the lucky ones. A van with parents and their three kids was involved, no one made it."

"That's rough."

I ran my hand over my face, then looked at my dad. "I'm not an asshole. I get why she's staying. It just—"

"Shocked you because it happened so fast."

"I guess. I could have handled it better than I did, though. But when she was talking and mentioned she didn't know when or if she'd be coming back... I told her there didn't seem much sense of us staying in touch then. I'd be busy with the club, and her focus needed to be on her mom and school anyway. Not much time left for the two of us." I grabbed a bag of chips off the counter and opened them.

11

"Crap, that's right, Raven's still in school."

"Yeah, only a few months left in this year. Guess if she stays, she'll finish high school there. She graduates next year." I chewed the chips I'd stuffed in my mouth, and when I looked at my dad, he was frowning. "What?"

"Easy to forget sometimes you aren't that old yourself, Reed. Hell, you're barely nineteen. And what's Raven, sixteen? Seventeen?" he asked.

"Seventeen, next month," I said and closed the bag of chips and placed them back on the counter. Raven had been my girl since I was in the eleventh grade, and she was a freshman.

"Maybe you could have handled the situation better, but I think you made the right decision for the both of you." I opened my mouth to speak, and my dad held his hand up and stopped me. "Before you get your back up, let me finish. Long distance relationships fail more times than they work. When they do work, it's usually because one of the parties willingly makes the sacrifice for the other. Like changing their job and relocating. You're still young. Raven especially. Neither of you need the pressure. Especially Raven. Living in a new place, attending a new school, and caring for her mom. That's a lot for her to take on. You are right, too—you will be busy with the club."

"I get what you're saying. Hell, I thought it. Right or wrong, breaking up with her was the right thing to do. I'm not going to lie, though. Thinking about her being so far away from me hurts, but her not coming back... It just

CM Books, LLC

seemed like the easiest way. So, I did the adult thing. But, Dad—"

"What, Reed?

"I've never considered my future where Raven wasn't a part of it."

"Aww, is Reed having girlfriend problems?" Sami, my teenage sister, said as she entered the kitchen, effectively ending the conversation with my dad.

"Hey, brat. Listening from the hallway?" I glared at her as she pulled a can of soda from the fridge, then grabbed the bag of chips I'd been eating off the counter.

"Nope, because takin' the time to eavesdrop would mean I care about what you have to say," Sami said, then shifted to face our dad. "Carly's coming over later, and we're going to watch movies. Is it alright if she stays the weekend?"

"Sure thing, princess."

"And that is my cue. I'm gonna leave you with the pain in the butt duo and head back to the clubhouse and enjoy the celebration." My dad smiled, and Sami stuck her tongue out at me.

"Enjoy yourself. Not every day you get patched in. And don't let some of the brothers put you to work."

I chuckled. "I won't. I did help with the setup, though, and the grill already had sizzling meat on it when I left. You sure you don't wanna at least ride over and grab something to eat?"

"Nah, I've got some files to look over that will keep me busy. It's why I didn't stick around after the patch-in. I'll

CM Books, LLC

throw some dinner together for the girls and me later. I can't leave Sami and Carly here alone to fend for themselves."

"We're not babies, and why can't we go to the clubhouse with you and eat? It's not like we're not there all the time."

"You and Carly have got no business at the clubhouse on Friday nights," my dad said, and I smirked when Sami huffed. As her older brother, it was my duty to pick on her any chance I got.

"That's right, brat, Friday night parties are for the grownups. *Children* are only allowed when there is a get-together for families." When Sami's eyes narrowed and she flipped me off, I laughed.

"Knock it off. Both of you." My dad looked between us and shook his head. "Stop picking on your sister," he said to me, then looked at Sami, who was sneering. "You, young lady, are not to be at the clubhouse on Friday nights. Period. And what have I told you about using the middle finger?"

"Yeah, yeah. I'm a girl. It isn't lady-like. Blah, blah," Sami said, rolled her eyes as only a girl hitting her teens could, then headed out of the kitchen. "At least I don't use any of the bad language I've heard my whole life. Besides, it's not like Friday nights are the only time boobs are flashed, or a penis is whipped out," she added before she was out of hearing distance.

I watched my dad's whole body stiffen. "Sami, your ass better be joking!" Our dad yelled and received giggles as an answer. His head dropped until his chin rested on his chest, then after a couple of deep breaths, he looked at me.

14

"Goddammit, if I make it until she's an adult with all my hair and what little sanity I have left, I want a damn party thrown for me. A big fucking one with a never-ending supply of booze until I can't remember a damn thing."

I snorted. "You got it, old man. Maybe you should have *the* talk with her. Again." I couldn't refrain from raggin' my dad.

He swiped his hand down his face. "Sure, 'cause that shit was so comfortable the first time around."

"Hey, I lived through it. Twice. I was ten the first time, and then for whatever reason, you felt the need to cover everything again a few years later."

"It's different between fathers and daughters. No man wants to discuss anything with his daughter that has to do with them turning into a woman. He doesn't want to acknowledge that one day he won't be the only man in her life."

"You do realize the chance of Sami ending up with a biker is almost a given since she's growing up around them."

"Don't damn go there. I try to keep those thoughts from entering my head right now. I'll deal with it when and if I'm faced with it and not a second before. The pool of denial I swim in is warm. Bad enough when we moved here and you were spending a lot of time at the clubhouse. I couldn't watch you twenty-four/seven, and the hang-arounds started looking at you as a fresh piece of meat when you were barely fourteen. Your hormones where surfacing big time and I didn't need their hormones added to the mix. So yeah, it was easier to have a sit down with you versus dealing with your

15

mama. Thank God she never noticed the looks those women threw your way. No doubt in my mind she would have clawed their eyes out." I watched the shadows move into his eyes, and the expression on his face change as it always did with the mention of my mother.

Mom had fought hard against the cancer that worked its way through her body, and in the end, when it finally won, my dad was left with two kids to raise. Dealing with her death had been an adjustment to the three of us. However, even with the club a heavy weight on my dad's shoulders, he spent as much time as possible with Sami and me.

"I have to say, I didn't mind the attention from the women." I wasn't able to keep the smirk away when I looked at my dad. Harassing him to lighten the mood was better than facing his sadness.

"I just bet your ass you didn't mind. I'm not so old I don't remember how teenage hormones take over leaving most males stupid. Don't forget I grew up in this club with scantily dressed women walking around every day and some with no issue of turning a teenage boy into a man."

"Weren't you thankful for several of 'em's lack of morals." I grinned as my dad shook his head.

"Get out of here. Go celebrate. Just be careful. Okay?"

"I will. I'll stay at the clubhouse if I need to. Try not to let Sami and Carly drive you nuts." I walked out of the kitchen smiling all the way to the front door as I listened to my dad gripe about girls turning into women and how he was more than likely going to spend his later years in prison

16

for murder. He was still bitching as I pulled the door closed behind me.

Once outside, I mounted my bike and headed in the direction of the clubhouse. The party would be a way for me to wash the remainder of my mood away.

Haven MC had felt like home to me since I walked into the clubhouse with my dad for the first time as a teenager. The club might be struggling with internal issues because some of the members felt my dad shouldn't be the president, but in my gut, I knew it was temporary. Wild Bill would make sure of it.

My dad left the military and moved us back when my mom was diagnosed with cancer, and his dad, my grandfather, the president of Haven at the time, was shot and killed on a run. It didn't matter to some that Haven was his legacy. They felt the vice president, Shock, who served under my grandfather, should be holding the president position.

When my dad stepped into the position of president, Shock and the few men who followed him weren't pleased. Even less pleased now that I'd been patched in.

Cleaning up the club would take time and I was more than ready to do my part to help my dad and brothers get it done. Haven MC would once again be strong and healthy under my dad's leadership.

I gave a chin lift to the two new prospects at the gate as I rode through and into the parking lot of the clubhouse. Bikes were lined up filling the lot, and the music blasting from inside could be heard over the sound of my pipes. As I parked, I thought of the club and the work it was going to

17

take from the other brothers and me to bring it back to its glory. Who had time to worry about a relationship in the first place? With that in mind, it settled in me that I'd done the right thing with Raven. Or I hoped that it was the right decision. Either way, it was over.

I entered the clubhouse and took the first steps to push Raven out of my head and move on when I sat down at the bar and started drinking. The more I drank, the decision to sever the relationship with Raven was the best option for both of us. Raven would realize that after she got over the initial hurt.

I ran a hand over my stomach, the ache in my gut I'm sure had to do with the liquor I was consuming. It had to be.

CM Books, LLC

Chapter One

Keg

"You're officially a property owner. How does it feel?" Mrs. Evans, the realtor who represented me in the purchase, said as we stepped out of the attorney's office into the stifling heat.

"No different than yesterday, Mrs. Evans. Except my bank account is significantly lighter today," I said as I walked toward the area in the lot where my bike and her car were parked.

"You snapped up the place under the appraised value. That alone should make you smile, hon."

"Oh, I've got no problem with the deal." We reached our vehicles, and I opened one of my saddlebags and placed my copy of the paperwork from the purchase inside.

Christ, I probably should have separated the bundle between both saddlebags, so one side wasn't heavier than the other. Who knew buying a house cost the earth a tree or

19

two? Not to mention the cramp in my hand from signing my name or initials more in one sitting than I had my whole life.

"Well, that's good enough for me. I enjoy it when my clients are pleased with their purchase." Mrs. Evans opened the door of her car and tossed her bag in. The door started to swing back on her and I moved to catch it. I held the door while she got behind the wheel and situated herself in the driver's seat.

"Appreciate all your help, Mrs. Evans. Drive safe."

"Such a sweet young man. Don't you let that beautiful home go to waste. It's too big for a single man. The place was built for a family. You should find yourself a good woman and fill the home with children."

I've been called several things in my life, but sweet was never one. I grinned at Mrs. Evans. "Now, what is Mr. Evans going to say when you tell him you're leaving him for me." I winked, and the older woman smiled, then threw back her head and laughed. I watched as she patted her hair, then ran her hands over her dress as if fixing it before she looked back at me. When she did, there was a gleam in her eyes.

"Hon, if I was thirty…hell, fifteen years younger, I'd take you for a ride or two."

My smile grew. "Mrs. Evans, I'm not sure I could handle you. You'd ruin me for other women, and then where would I be when you up and left me?"

"Please. I highly doubt you've ever had a problem finding a female to keep you company. Now get out of here and go enjoy your house."

"Plan to," I said and pushed the button on the door, locking her car door, then stepped back.

"I bet you will. Just remember what I said. Find a good a woman and make that house into a home," Mrs. Evans said, then pulled the car door closed. I waited until she drove out of the parking lot before getting on my bike and doing the same.

Making my way up the driveway, I looked over the front of my house with its wraparound porch and could picture myself relaxing there in the evening. It was one of the reasons I'd chosen the house. Parking in front of the steps that led onto the porch, I pulled the keys out of my pocket on my way to the front door. I smiled as I pushed the door open. The place might be empty at the moment, but it was mine.

The open floor plan had been another draw for me. I walked through the downstairs until I stood in the kitchen, looking out the windows from the eat-in area into the backyard. I still couldn't believe the place was mine as I watched the water ripple in the pool from the wind. Passed the pool, there was more lawn and an outbuilding set off to one side that was built to match the look of the house. Behind the shed, the mowed lawn turned into a wooded area untouched and giving the house privacy from the property on the other side of it.

After checking out the master suite on the first floor, I made my way upstairs and walked down the hall, looking into each of the four bedrooms and the two bathrooms.

21

Before heading back downstairs, I stopped and looked over the railing into the family room below.

Standing there taking in the enormousness of the house, I briefly wondered what I was thinking of buying a five bedroom, three and a half bath house. I could only imagine what my brothers were going to say when they saw it. I hadn't mentioned to anyone about buying a house. I hadn't even told my dad I was looking for one.

I walked down the stairs, grabbed one of the three garage door openers off the island in the kitchen, and headed back to the front door. Once outside and on my bike, I rode toward the clubhouse. With most of my stuff at my apartment packed, I needed to round up some of the brothers to help me move it to the house. No time like the present to break the news.

Mac, the prospect working the gate, lifted his chin as I pulled up to and through the gate at Haven MC's clubhouse. A few members were outside talking to a woman and little girl when I backed my bike up. But that wasn't unusual, nor what grabbed my attention, it was the kid who walked around inspecting the bikes lined up beside mine. I dismounted and headed toward the boy who stood beside Pinch's bike admiring the dual chrome pipes. When I saw his hand reach out, I picked up my pace.

"Hey, be careful, they might still be hot," I said as I reached him.

"Is it yours?" the kid asked as he looked up at me. He was young, but tall. His hair was dark brown and long

22

enough that one side fell across his face causing him to swing his head to shift it out of his eyes.

"Nah, mine's the one on the end," I pointed toward my bike, "this one belongs to my brother, Pinch. You like it?" I asked and saw the gleam in his brown eyes as he smiled.

"Yeah, it is freakin' awesome. The paint job on the gas tank is wicked, especially the skull. Did he buy the bike like that?" I wanted to laugh at the excitement in the kid's voice. But hell, I knew how the boy felt. I still remembered the feeling from the first time I straddled a bike. Nothing compared, and it only had gotten better when I'd taken off on the bike, and the wind hit me. The only other time I could recall feeling anything remotely close was maybe the first time I had sex. But considering the awkwardness of my first experience with sex—riding for the first time still ranked first.

I'd never seen the kid around the club before, so I knew he didn't belong to any of the brothers. Unless someone's family was visiting that had never been to the clubhouse before.

The kid stared at me, and I realized I hadn't answered his question. "No. He bought the bike, added a few things to it, then had the tank painted."

"Man, it's cool," he said and leaned closer to the Haven emblem painted on the side of the tank.

"You like bikes, huh?" When he glanced over his shoulder at me, I imagined the look on his face was the same one every kid had when around motorcycles.

23

"Oh, yeah. I'm trying to talk my mom into letting me get a dirt bike. I could ride it at the house. There's plenty of woods, but she says I'm not old enough. Geez, she treats me like a baby. I want to practice and get used to riding for when I'm old enough to own a motorcycle."

I bit the inside of my cheek to keep from chuckling when he rolled his eyes. Damn, I didn't envy his parents with his attitude.

"What's your name, kid?" I asked as he continued to examine Pinch's bike, checking out every detail.

He answered without even looking at me. "Ryker Allen. Everyone calls me Ry. Well, except my grandpa, but he's old."

"Okay, Ry, it is." I chuckled, then snorted when his name registered. "How much shit you catch with that name?" I asked because no way the parents didn't realize what they were doing when they named him.

The kid stood and grinned. "At first, a lot. Then I just started telling people that my mom named me after the prison 'Ryker Island' because my dad was serving time there when I was born," Ry sneered, and I laughed. "Kids are gullible."

I shook my head. "You realize you're a kid, right?"

Ry hit me with a full-blown smile that showed teeth with braces. "Yep, but I'm smarter. Plus, you'd be surprised how many kids don't know about Ryker Island."

"I have no doubt, kid." I grinned back at him. I didn't have a lot of experience with kids. Especially teenage ones. Closest I came to kids was my niece, Ally. And she was a

24

riot. I already felt sorry for Sami and Speed when the girl hit puberty. Ry was easy to like, enough so, I found myself curious to whom he belonged. "You here with your parents?"

"Just my mom."

"Oh. You related to one of my brothers?"

The kid frowned. "Brothers?"

"Related to one of the guys in the club. Brother is how we refer to each other."

"Oh, I get it. But no, we don't know anyone here. A call came into my grandad's clinic about a sick snake and he sent my mom here. My little sister and I came with her." I looked over my shoulder, following where the kid pointed to the woman and little girl.

"Your mom a vet?"

"Yep. She normally doesn't deal with reptiles. Before we moved here, she mostly worked with large animals, like horses and cows. Here she's going to be treating all kinds of animals, even reptiles. Reagan went inside with her. She likes snakes." From the look of disgust that crossed Ry's face, I assumed he didn't care much for snakes or the fact that his sister wasn't bothered by them.

"Problem with snakes?"

"The things creep me out. Even the black ones that hang around and eat mice." Ry cringed.

"I'm with you there, kid. Not fond of those things myself."

"Guess I better go before my mom yells for me," Ry said and moved around me. I turned and followed so I could

25

check in with Freak. Evidently, one of the man's snakes had taken ill. He took better care of his snakes than he did himself most of the time.

Ry's mom stood with her back to me and held the hand of a little dark-haired girl while she talked with a few of my brothers. She was dressed in jeans, a t-shirt, and boots. And the woman filled out the jeans. If the front matched the back, Ry's dad was one lucky man.

"Hey, Mom," Ry said just as we reached the group. When the woman and the little girl turned—I was left speechless as a piece of my past met my eyes.

I stared at the woman I hadn't seen since she was going on seventeen. As she looked back at me, I noticed the years had been good to her. Her black hair was pulled into a ponytail and left her face on full display. As a young girl, she had been beautiful, but as a grown woman, gorgeous didn't even seem a good enough of a description.

Talking had ceased around us, and I didn't need to glance away to know my brothers watched us.

"It's good to see you, Reed."

Chapter Two

Raven

I thought I'd prepared myself to face Reed. How wrong I was. When Gramps called my cell and asked me to handle the call he'd received from Mr. Owens about his snake being lethargic, I agreed to the house call before I was informed on where he lived. I knew the location of the Haven MC's clubhouse, everyone in town and the surrounding area did. But I'd never spent time there when Reed and I dated. Our time together was spent either at his house or mine.

Gramps knew what he asked of me, and I could have argued about not being ready to face any confrontation, but there was no way around it. I didn't want to have an argument with him on the phone since the kids were in the car with me. And definitely not one pertaining to Reed.

Moving back to the area, I hadn't expected to avoid Reed forever. It'd never been my intention, but I had hoped for more time. Time to come to terms with what needed to

CM Books, LLC

be done. Time before the choice I made so long ago came into question. Time to steel myself for Reed's hatred when the truth was revealed. Because there was no doubt that he would hate me. And he would have the right to.

As I drove to the Haven MC's compound, I prayed luck continued to be on my side as it had before every time I visited my grandparents over the years. Being honest with myself, it was probably due more to me avoiding trips into town so I wouldn't cross his path.

I'd almost made it today. I probably would have if a few of the men hadn't followed me out to inquire about Mr. Owen's—Freak as he asked me to call him—snake.

When I turned at Ry's voice and saw Reed standing beside him, all I could do was stare. Reed's expression likely mimicked mine as we both stood speechless. One of shock.

Once I noticed the sound around us had stopped, I gathered myself enough to speak, "It's good to see you, Reed."

"Raven. Been a while," Reed said as he looked me up and down with blue eyes so familiar to me. Eyes set in a chiseled face framed by hair a little darker than the sandy blond I remembered. I sometimes saw those eyes in dreams. Dreams I hated. Dreams that reminded me of a time I needed to forget. My first love. My first heartbreak.

"Mom, you've got to see the bikes before we leave," Ry said, unsuspecting of the tension in the air around him.

I forced my eyes away from Reed and looked at my son. "You didn't touch any of them, did you?" I asked while fighting for enough composure to get me through the

28

encounter. I needed to delay the overdue discussion with Reed even for one more day. I wanted to have the discussion on my terms. But my gramps could very well have taken it out of my hands.

Ry sighed, "Come on, Mom. I know not to touch a guy's ride. I'm not stupid. Geez." Ry looked at Reed as he swung his head to the side to get the too long hair, which was in bad need of a trim, out of his eyes. "Women, they just don't understand that guys are protective of their rides."

I glanced at Reed and noticed his lips twitching while the men behind me didn't even try to hide their response and laughed. "Ry, you have several years before you'll need to worry about that."

"It's not that long. Besides, time goes by fast. At least that's what you say every year on your birthday."

"Ry," I said wearily as Reed chuckled. Evidently, he had no problem laughing at my expense.

It was hard for me, but I refrained from rolling my eyes because this had been an ongoing conversation from the first time Ry had seen a motorcycle. He'd been fascinated and talked nonstop about having one. And with the move back to my grandparents' place and all the land surrounding their house, he'd started pushing extra hard for a dirt bike. After today, I was sure Ry would up his game even more with not-so-subtle hints on how his life would be better if he had a dirt bike to ride. I'd been able to push off getting him a bike or four-wheeler for the last year, now…it was just a matter of when I gave in to him. I couldn't let my fear bleed on to him.

29

Before I could tell Ry it wasn't the time nor place to have this discussion, Reed leaned into Ry and lowered his voice, "Working way too hard to sell it, buddy."

"You don't know her, she won't give. Kids younger than me ride dirt bikes. She wouldn't even let me have a four-wheeler where we lived before and all my friends had them."

"She's not those other kids' mom. She's yours. And I'm sure she has her reasons, so why not cut her a break?"

My stomach tightened, and I felt an ache under my left breast as I watched the interaction between Ry and Reed. Especially when Ry looked up at Reed with a noticeable look of respect, maybe even a little awe, in his eyes and agreed with him easily, instead of continuing to rant. "Yeah…okay."

The pain and regret I was feeling were placed on hold when Reagan decided she'd been quiet long enough.

"If I can't have a dog, butthead can't have a dirt bike." I looked down at Reagan as she stared up at me, then added, "Right, Momma?"

I closed my eyes and took a deep breath while chuckles surrounded me. My children's manners were off on a break, so it seemed.

Anyone who says parenting is easy doesn't have kids, or they have nannies who handle most of the raising while they participate when the mood strikes them.

"Reagan, what have I told you about calling your brother names?" I opened my eyes and lifted a brow at my daughter, whose facial expression told me she was contemplating her reply.

"Well…you said not to, but he calls me fart face when you're not around. And that's not nice."

I silently wished the ground would open beneath me, but that would require some luck. And it was more than apparent to me that I must be out of my quota for the day. Left with nothing else, I shifted to the side so I could see the men who I'd turned my back on when Ry called out to me. Once everyone was in view, I apologized, "I'm sorry. I swear they don't normally act like this."

"No reason to apologize. Name calling between siblings is natural. It's almost a rite of passage between siblings," Pinch, the one who had met me in the parking lot when I first arrived, said while the other two men beside him nodded in agreement.

"Good to know. Being an only child, I didn't get to partake in that experience. Though, I often wonder what having a sibling would have been like."

"A pain," Reed replied. "Sami and I used to go back and forth enough that Wild Bill threatened both of us with military school. Still," Reed looked down at Ry before he continued, "even though my sister and I give each other a hard time, there's nothing we wouldn't do for one another. And part of being a big brother is that you watch over your sister. Understand?"

"Yes, sir. You're saying I can pick on her for bugging me, but others can't." I smiled at Ry. The respectful kid seemed to have reappeared.

I continued to smile as I thought about Reed's sister. Sami always wanted to hang around us and Reed would run her off. She'd call him a few choice names, then huff and stomp away mumbling how she'd get even with him. Which she did quite often.

"Hell, Keg, you still argue with Sami."

"Really, Pinch, like you and Madison don't?"

"That's because Madison doesn't listen to dick."

Before I got the chance to remind the two men about young ears being present, Reagan proved that kids don't miss much when she asked, "Who's Dick?"

Both men stopped talking and glanced at me, then down at Reagan as if they'd forgotten she was there. Instead of waiting to see how the men would answer, I used the pause in the conversation to try to make an escape.

"Well, we should be on our way. We've taken up enough of your time. It was nice meeting everyone," I said as I looked between Reed and the others.

"You, too, Raven. And thanks for getting here so quickly. I know Freak appreciated it. Not to mention, you're much better to look at than old Doc Newhouse," Pinch said, then winked.

"Any time. Wish I could have had more answers for Mr. Owens, but my knowledge of rattlesnakes is slim. It really could be as simple as a bad meal, or it is reaching the end of its lifespan." I shrugged my shoulders. "It's a guessing game."

"Yeah, I heard Freak say he's owned it for twenty years, and it wasn't a baby when he caught it," Pinch said, and I nodded.

"They typically have a lifespan in the wild of roughly twenty-five years give or take. In captivity, they have been known to reach well into the thirties, though. And there really isn't a way to estimate their age either. Counting the rattles on the tail isn't an accurate measure."

"Damn, I hope it's feeling bad from a bad mouse because if it croaks, Freak will be a mess," Reed said.

"Not going to be a pretty sight, brother," Pinch answered Reed, then turned to the men beside him. "Guess we should check on Freak. He'll worry himself sick over this."

The other men nodded, and without another word, they turned and went inside, leaving Ry, Reagan, and myself standing with Reed.

There was a long pause before Reed finally spoke, "It was a surprise seeing you here, and it didn't click when I first walked up that you were the vet. You helping your grandad out while you're visiting?" Reed asked.

"Mom's taking over for Gramps. He's retiring," Ry answered before I could.

"That so?" One of Reed's brows lifted as he looked at me. So much for my attempt to escape.

I didn't want to notice how good Reed looked. But it was hard not to. So instead of fighting it, I looked him up and down. He hadn't changed as much as he filled out from the young man I remembered. He was a little taller, and his body was more muscular. Not that he hadn't been in shape at nineteen, it's that his t-shirts had never strained against his chest like the one he was wearing under his vest. His hair was shorter and slightly darker, but the waves remained. The most noticeable change was the tiny lines on the outside corners of his eyes. His face was harder and more pronounced, too. Then again, my own features held changes from the young girl I was before I moved away. And with what Ry, Reagan and I had been through in the last year, I'm surprised my own face wasn't covered with worry lines. Derek's sudden death was hard on the three of us. And while work gave me a small reprieve while coping, Ry and Reagan were left with each other and adjusting to not have Derek around.

A tug on my arm snapped me out of my head and I looked down at Reagan. "Can I go with Ry?"

I frowned, realizing that while I'd cataloged the changes in Reed's appearance, I hadn't answered him and missed something with the kids. "Go where with Ry?"

"Geez, Mom, we asked like ten times. Can we go look at the bikes while you're talking?" Ry said.

"Not quite sure it was ten, pal. Maybe three," Reed said and chuckled. "You took a little side trip, Raven."

Of course, he not only noticed, but he would also have to mention it, too. Heat rose with my embarrassment from being caught. I chose to ignore Reed and answered Ry instead, "Go ahead but stay close. We need to leave soon." Reagan let go of my hand and started walking away with Ry. "Look only, Reagan. No touching."

"She'll be fine, Raven. Not like she can take off on one of them. Her legs aren't long enough to touch the ground."

"Funny, Reed," I said dryly.

He smirked and shook his head. "So, you're working with Doc? Can't believe he's thinking of retiring."

"Yes, he is. Once I familiarize myself with his practice, he's going to retire. At least that's what he says. Even if he shocks me and does retire, I don't expect him to stay away. He'll find some excuse to stop in, I'm sure. He'll want to see if I'm handling his clients with care."

"You always talked about wanting to be a vet. I'm glad to see you made your dream a reality." Reed glanced down and then back up. "I'm sure your grandparents love having you and your husband and kids around."

I realized then what he looked for when he glanced down. It took everything in me not to run my finger over the simple band. If I weren't holding the medical bag with my left hand, I probably would have. Even though it had been a year since I lost Derek, I hadn't been able to remove the ring.

Afraid to go down that route for fear of bringing on tears, I focused on the conversation. "Working with animals was all I ever wanted to do. Easiest decision I've ever made."

"Yeah, some decisions are easy, while others are a lot harder to make." Something flashed in Reed's eyes, but before I could identify it, it was gone as quickly as it surfaced.

"We needed a change, so when Gramps mentioned retiring, it seemed the perfect opportunity," I said, and Reed's eyes squinted. He opened his mouth just as a buzz sounded, stopping whatever he was going to say.

Reed pulled a cell phone from his pocket and glanced down at the screen. Not prepared to explain further on my need for change, I took his distraction as an opportunity to be on my way. The longer I was left alone with him, the chance of a slip happening that would cause a scene I wasn't ready to deal with.

I stepped around Reed, leaving him to answer his call in private, and called out to my kids. "Ry, Reagan, time to go."

Both kids turned and started walking in my direction. "Can we stop and get some food? I'm hungry," Reagan asked.

"Sure thing, honey," I answered as we started across the lot. When we reached the car, Ry got in the passenger side while Reagan got in the back. After I doubled checked that she had fastened her seatbelt correctly, I closed her door and opened the driver's side one. Just as I prepared to get in, I heard footsteps and turned.

"Is something wrong?" I asked as Reed approached us.

"No, wanted to say goodbye and that it was nice running into you, Rav," Reed said, then bent and leaned in my open door. "It was nice meeting you guys, too."

"I'm not a guy, I'm a girl," Reagan said from the backseat, and I sighed. At seven, Reagan took everything literally and had no qualms about voicing anything that popped into her mind.

CM Books, LLC

Reed chuckled. "My mistake, sweetheart," he said, and received a smile from Reagan before he stood back up. "Bet she's a handful?"

"And beyond," I said on a sigh.

"If she's anything like Ally, I can imagine your life is anything but dull."

Before I could stop myself, I asked, "Is Ally your daughter?"

The tiny lines at the corners of Reed's eyes became more prominent as a full-blown smile crested his face. "No, she's my five-year-old niece. And calling her a handful doesn't even come close to describing her."

"Oh my gosh, Sami has a child?" I asked with a tad bit too much exuberance while the knotted feeling in my stomach I'd gotten when he first mentioned Ally, dissolved. That reaction would need to be evaluated, and it was something to do when I was alone. Not while standing in front of the man who caused the reaction.

"Yeah, Ally and another on the way."

"That's so great. Time sure does go by fast."

"Not always."

When Reed nor I said anything else, several seconds of uncomfortable silence ensued and would have continued if not thankfully, for the impatience of my children.

"Momma, I'm really hungry," Reagan yelled from the back.

"Guess that's my cue," I said as I looked at Reed, then shifted and got into my car. When I reached for the handle,

Reed stepped back and stood in place while I pulled my door shut, started the car and rolled my window down.

Once I backed out from the spot, I gave Reed a small wave. He lifted his chin, then said, "See ya around, Rav."

I nodded, then turned my head to look at the kids. "Who's ready for some burgers?" I asked as I slipped the car in drive.

"'Bout time. I thought I was going to turn thirteen before I got to eat lunch!" Ry said, and I laughed as I gave the car gas.

As we reached the gate, I heard, "Stop them!" Then the biker, who stood off to the side of the gate, moved until he stood in front of my car. I hit the brakes, and after the car stopped and I saw how close I was to the biker, I closed my eyes and blew out a breath. When I opened my eyes, I glanced in the rearview mirror and saw Reed jogging toward the gate.

"Holy sh—cow!" Ry shouted.

"Language, Ryker," I said more out of habit than I actually cared about correcting him on his near slip right at that moment. Probably because I wanted to say worse.

"Why is the man in front of our car?" Reagan asked, and I looked over my shoulder to make sure she was okay since slamming down on the brakes jerked us. She was leaning over as far as her belt would allow so she could see between the seats and out the windshield at the biker who I'm sure would've been flattened if I'd been one second slower slamming my foot down on the brake petal.

I leaned my head out the window as Reed approached my car window. "I hope there's a good reason for this," I said as I waved my hand toward the biker that stood to block me from exiting.

"Probably a better fucking reason than you have." With the tone of Reed's voice, I snapped my eyes to his and the coldness reflected at me sent a shiver down my spine.

Almost immediately, the question of what could have happened to have him pissed off came to mind.

"I don't understand, Reed."

"See if this jars anything. Before you pulled away, I heard Ry's comment about turning thirteen," he sneered.

The two minutes from when I backed out of the parking space and reached the gate would be remembered as the calm before the storm. And the simple statement from Ry didn't unravel my betrayal. It shredded it.

CM Books, LLC

Chapter Three

Keg

Betrayed, hurt, angry, cheated. Every one of those emotions flooded me as I stood there focused on Raven. When she realized I knew—nothing—not even the moisture that filled her eyes could keep me from raging. If anything, I felt my anger grow.

I had enjoyed talking with Raven earlier. At least after the initial shock passed from seeing her at the club. During the encounter with her and her kids, I briefly wondered how different my life would be if she'd stayed or even kept in touch.

Even as I watched her prepare to drive away, a strange contentment washed over me that I hadn't felt for a long time. Not since before she'd moved away if I was honest with myself. I'd smiled when I heard the kids through her open window answer her question on picking up food.

Then she waved and started pulling away when Ry's statement, *I thought I was going to turn thirteen before I got to eat*

41

lunch, registered. And the next thing I knew, I was jogging toward the gate yelling for Mac to stop them.

How quickly one's life would change.

"I planned to tell you. I just…" Raven said as she looked at me and a tear slid from the corner of her eye.

I looked toward Ry and saw him with new eyes. The resemblance to my dad, and Sami since she favored Wild Bill, was there if you looked. His face was at the in between stages of youth, where the softness in the area around the cheeks was changing, and the bone structure was becoming more prominent. He had my chin for God's sake.

"When were you planning to tell me that I had a son? As he went off to college, when he married? Did you have a timeline worked out on sharing the information?" I threw the questions at her, and my voice rose with each one.

"Oh damn," came from Mac while Raven continued to stare with tears freely rolling down her cheeks then.

I was so deep into my anger that I hadn't heard the approach of several motorcycles until they reached the entrance to the Haven. With Raven's vehicle taking up most of the space, the bikes passed single file.

By the time the last bike passed, I was done with Raven's silence. "Answer me, goddammit! When were you going to tell me about my son!" I screamed and slammed my hands down on the top of the car.

Several things occurred after that move to have my anger dialed down a few notches. Raven jumped and scooted away from the door, whether it just scared her or if she expected me to hit her next. From the backseat, Reagan burst into tears, and the shocked wide-eyed look on Ry's face as he stared at me was a cold splash of ice water on my temper.

Could I have handled the situation any worse?

I added disgust to my feelings. Appalled at my actions. What type of man exploded at a woman—and frightened two children?

"Son, I think that's enough for right now." My dad's hand clasped down on my shoulder and squeezed. When I turned my head to look at him, I noticed the brothers who rode in with him, stood off to the side.

Nothing like showing your ass with an audience.

I shook my head and dropped my hands from the car roof. After I stepped back, I looked at Mac and jerked my head to the side. He gave a chin lift in acknowledgment and moved to the side, unblocking Raven's car.

Raven swiped at her cheeks and spoke softly to Reagan, assuring the little girl everything would be okay. Ry had straightened in the passenger seat and stared out the windshield, not saying a word. I'd give anything to know what was running through his head. Then again, after my actions, maybe it was best I didn't.

I took a deep breath and ran my hand down my face. "We need to talk, Raven, and as much as I want answers, I can't deal with you right now. You can leave."

"Reed, I'm so sorry. I wanted…"

I ignored her attempt to apologize. "I'll be by your grandparents' place tomorrow afternoon. I expect answers then. Make sure you're there, too. I don't want to hunt you down, but I will if you aren't there." I turned my back on Raven, dislodging my dad's hand in the process, and started walking toward the clubhouse.

The timbre of my dad's voice reached my ears along with Raven's, but I couldn't make out what they said. When I reached where my brothers stood, they parted, and as I passed by, each one reached out and squeezed my shoulder.

As I reached the clubhouse entrance, I looked back and saw Raven pulling out and the others getting on their bikes. I didn't bother to wait on them. I swung the door open and entered, then headed into the main room. I passed brothers with no acknowledgment, my focus set on the bar. A drink was needed, the alcohol would go a long way when I had to rehash what had gone down. No way would my dad let that shit show go unexplained.

"A little early for the hard stuff, brother," Pinch said as he sat on the barstool beside me.

I gave him the side-eye before I picked up the glass of whiskey I poured and downed it. Picking up the bottle that I left on the bar, I refilled my glass.

"Not sharing what's crawled up your ass? Had to happen between the time I left you outside with the doc and when you walked in here."

"You could be a cop with those detective skills," I sneered.

"You're such an asshole, Keg."

"Yet, you're sitting here trying to fuck with me."

I heard my dad's voice as he and the others entered the clubhouse. Tipping the glass in my hand back, I

44

swallowed the last of the liquid before slamming the glass down on the bar. Both Pinch and I stood when Wild Bill walked in, followed by Moose, Crank, and Tram.

Wild Bill lifted his arm and checked his watch, then looked back up and straight at me. "Keg, my office."

The others stayed in the main room as I pushed away from the bar and followed my dad. Once inside his office, he sat behind his desk as I took one of the seats in front of it.

"You know what makes you a good enforcer?"

"I don't have a problem smacking heads together."

"I'll give you that. But the main reason is your ability to stay calm in situations until you've assessed everything going on before you let your temper take over. You've got a nasty temper when it surfaces, son." Wild Bill raised his hand to stop me before I could speak. "I get the reason behind your explosion but, son, not only was that unusual for you to snap before getting answers, you've never treated a woman like what I witnessed."

"Never had a woman keep my son away from me for twelve fucking years before." I no longer could stay quiet. "I stood outside talking with Raven with my son standing beside me and didn't know it. Hell, I had a conversation with the kid before I even knew she was at the clubhouse and his mother. And I still wouldn't know if I hadn't overheard the kid mention his age. How can you sit there so damn calm about this? He's not only my son, he's your grandson!" I bent my head, then ran my hand across my neck to try to ease the tension I felt building once again.

"Because screaming and yelling won't change the fact. That's why. The past is done, Reed, it's how you handle going forward that's going to count. And exploding over what is done may make you feel better, but it doesn't change dick."

"Twelve, Dad! Twelve years I can't get back."

"No, you can't. I know you're hurt and angry. You've got every right to be, Reed. You'll get no argument from me there. But it isn't just about you. After you walked away, I spoke with Raven and made sure she was good to drive. The boy didn't say a word the whole time she talked with me. The expression on his face was blank. I'm not sure the boy knew either, or if he did know before, he didn't know it was you."

"Raven admitted to you the boy *is* mine? Because she never came right out and answered me. She only said she was sorry. Sorry for keeping my son a secret. Who the fuck does that and then thinks sorry makes it all better? It's like putting a band-aid on an open chest wound." I looked at my dad and saw sympathy in his eyes, which made my pain three times worse.

"Yes. She admitted you are his dad. She also knows she screwed up. Knows you're angry and has accepted that you won't ever forgive her. She doesn't want you to hold what she did against Ry, though, because she's hurt him too."

"So you think the kid didn't have a clue that her husband isn't his real dad? At least until I blurted out I was. Fuck, I even made the little girl cry." I pinched my nose at

46

the point between my eyes and took several deep breaths. "When I heard Ry and it registered with me that he had to be mine, a red haze covered my eyes, and I just acted." I paused while everything that had happened settled in me. And as always, my dad stayed quiet, waiting, giving me the time to come to terms with it all. "Shit, Dad, I've got a kid."

He grinned. "Yeah, you do. Aren't you glad you bought a house? Be a lot easier to get the kid to spend time with you if he has his own space."

I lifted a brow and shook my head. Why I thought I could keep anything from the man. "Should I even bother asking how you found out?"

My dad's grin widened, then a couple raps on the door had him yelling, "Open!" When he looked at me again, he said, "You're my son. I know everything that goes on with you?"

Before I could reply the door opened. "Not everything, Prez," Moose said as he, Pinch, Crank, and Tram walked in.

"What the hell are you talking about, Moose?" my dad asked as the guys grabbed chairs and sat down.

"Well, evidently, a little over twelve years ago, give or take a few months, you didn't know Keg knocked up his teenage girlfriend."

I glared at Moose, but Pinch's response, "Christ, Moose, you're an asshole," had me shaking my head again while the other brothers chuckled.

"Hey, a little while ago, you called me an asshole," I said, then chuckled when Pinch's eyes narrowed.

47

"Well, you both are. But I think Moose edges you out as the biggest."

"And where do you fall on the asshole scale?" Crank joined in, and Pinch glared at him.

"Don't start shit with me because I caught you flirting with Mad," Pinch sneered at Crank.

"I wasn't flirting. I was at the counter taking out some cash! Besides, your sister is a grown woman. She's the one who walked up to me," Crank said. At the mention of the bank, it cleared up how my dad knew I bought a house. Pinch's sister works there. She probably figured my brothers knew and had mentioned something to Pinch.

"Don't make me kick your ass. I've told you to stay away from Mad."

My lips twitched at Pinch's words. Crank and Pinch were best friends and had been since grade school. But it didn't matter when it came to Pinch's sister. Best friend or not, he didn't want Crank around Madison. Hell, he didn't want any of the brothers around Madison.

It didn't escape me that watching them go back and forth gave me the time I needed to let loose of the remaining anger I held. Tomorrow I'd get my answers regardless if I liked them or not. When it was over, no matter my feelings toward Raven, I'd work on getting to know my son.

"Like you could," Crank said, and he and Pinch both stood facing off with each other.

"Either one of you throws a punch and I will personally kick *both* your asses. Sit the hell down!" At my

48

dad's reprimand, a few seconds passed as the two stared at each other before finally reoccupying their seats.

Wild Bill relaxed and leaned back in his chair. "For Christ's sake, what the hell is wrong with you boys?"

"I'd suggest they'd regressed back to grade school but, Prez, you don't look much like any teacher I ever had," Tram said, and his lips twitched.

I laughed at the image Tram's statement brought on. And just like that, the tension in the room was gone. Nothing beat the camaraderie of my brothers.

"Enough goofing off. We've got some business to deal with. Hawk will be here soon. He was waiting on Charlie," Prez said.

"Yeah, they were five minutes out when he called. That's why we came to the office," Moose said.

"This have to do with the text you sent earlier, Prez?" I asked.

Prez leaned forward and rested his forearms on his desk. "Part of it. I'll catch you all up when Hawk arrives. No sense having to repeat myself."

CM Books, LLC

Chapter Four

Raven

The kids and I sat in the car in front of my grandparents' house. Ry nor Reagan had spoken since I pulled away from Haven. Not even a peep when I stopped at the burger place and pulled through their drive-thru. No one shouted out what they wanted when it was our turn to order.

Never in any of the scenarios over the years when I thought about telling Reed about Ry—did today's episode run through my mind. I anticipated his temper and that he might feel betrayed, but when faced with all the emotions pushing out from him today, being prepared was nowhere close.

Placing my hand on my chest where my heart was, I could almost physically feel its hurt. The beat may have been regular, but I wonder if the organ was left with a crack.

I steeled my spine, blew out a breath and grabbed the handle on the driver's side door. Sitting in the car surrounded by silence wasn't going to change what happened or what was still to come. And it was a little too late to run.

"Ry, Reagan, come on. Let's go inside. The food is getting cold."

Ry unbuckled his belt, then got out of the car. "I'm not hungry," he said without looking at me. I watched as he walked to the porch, climbed the three steps, then walked inside.

I opened Reagan's door and helped her out. "Mommy? How can Ry have two daddies? Do I have two daddies, too?" Reagan's questions at least gave me insight on why she hadn't spoken on the drive home. She'd been too busy wrapping her seven-year-old brain around everything she'd witnessed.

Reaching back inside the car for the food, I thought of how I could explain it to her. "No, sweetie, you only have one daddy. Ry, well…he… has a daddy and I guess a stepdaddy." I raised up with the food bags in hand and looked down at Reagan, her eyebrows were drawn together, and she was chewing on her lower lip. God, I was screwing it all up.

"Then, I want a stepdaddy."

"Oh, sweetie, it doesn't work that way." I closed the car door, and with my free hand, pulled my daughter to my side. "Let's go inside and eat, and I promise I'll try to explain it so you can understand. Okay?"

"Alright," Reagan said and sighed as we walked to the porch. "The man scared me when he yelled and hit the car.

Is he a mean man?" Reagan whispered, and I barely made out what she said.

Stopping our progress, I turned Reagan to face me, then stooped to her level. "Men get mad and raise their voices. They even hit stuff sometimes, though they shouldn't. And a man should *never* hit a woman period. You get mad and yell at Ry when he picks on you, right?"

"Uh huh."

"So you understand that just because Reed was mad and raised his voice, it doesn't make him a bad person?"

"Were you scared of him?" Her small voice broke my heart.

"The noise when he hit the car made me jump. But it wasn't because I was afraid of him."

"Oh."

I wanted to reassure Reagan and tell her she could trust Reed never to physically hurt her. But words hurt, too. Reagan needed to decide for herself where Reed was concerned. He'd scared her, and it would be up to him to prove to her that even angry he'd never harm her or anyone else.

"Come on, sweetie." We continued walking and when we reach the steps to the porch, the front door opened and my grandmother stepped outside.

"Everything okay out here?" I wondered if she'd ran into Ry or gotten one of her feelings. Growing up, it was uncanny sometimes how she *just felt* something was wrong.

There was no reason to avoid her question, my eyes surely showed signs of my recent crying. "I made a house call today."

"Alright…"

"At the Haven MC's clubhouse," I said as I reached for the handle on the front door. Reagan went inside after I pushed it open. "And Reed was there."

"Oh, honey," Gran said as she and I stepped inside, shutting the door behind us.

"May I watch TV while I eat?" Reagan asked as we entered the kitchen and I set the bags on the table.

"Sure, sweetie." I pulled the food out of the bags and followed Reagan into the living room. While I set her up at the coffee table, Gran brought a drink in for her.

Once Reagan was settled, I returned to the kitchen, pulled a chair out, and sat. After pouring two glasses of tea, Gran joined me at the table.

"Go ahead and say I told you so."

"You know I'd never do that."

"Why not, Gran? From the start, both you and Gramps were against me keeping the pregnancy from Reed." I rubbed my forehead as if it would relieve the headache that was beginning.

"Yes, we were."

"Yet you stood by my decision. In a way, I wish you would have pressured me into telling him. I was so naïve to think I would be able to keep it a secret. And even more that I've kept it for this long. Now, when I look back, it was harder work trying to keep it from him every time I came to

CM Books, LLC

visit than if I'd told Reed, and he hadn't cared and stepped away. Which was one of the reasons I told myself to justify not telling him. I'm not sure I would have been able to take his rejection. Then again, at least it would have been his choice not to be involved. Do you know how many times I've asked myself if the decision to tell him now was because Derek is gone? If he was still living, would I have kept the truth hidden?"

"Only you can answer those questions. But you were seventeen when you found out you were pregnant, Raven. Your boyfriend had broken up with you. You moved across the country to help your mother. Stephanie is my daughter and I will always love her, but it doesn't keep me from getting mad at her. I know she was behind you staying there permanently."

"Gran, she needed the help to recover, and no way could Jacob help her with all the traveling for his job."

"Bullshit!" she said loudly.

"Gran!" I scolded, then look toward the living room, and thankfully Reagan was engrossed in her television show and wasn't paying attention to us.

"Don't Gran me. I know Stephanie needed assistance in the beginning. She and Jacob could have paid someone to help her after we left, a more qualified caretaker than her seventeen-year-old daughter. It had nothing to do with money either. They could afford it. Even before your Gramps and I were ready to return home, we offered to pay for a live-in nurse until she was able to get around on her own. She turned us down. I told her you needed to get back to your life and were too young to take on the burden of caring for her. That's when she said Jacob wasn't comfortable with the idea of some unknown person living in their home. Especially since he wouldn't be around much to keep an eye on them." My Gran rolled her eyes. "He wasn't worried they might kill Stephanie in her sleep. No, he was worried someone might steal from them."

It felt good to smile. My Gran was something else. "You never liked him, did you, Gran?"

The woman didn't even have to think about it. She immediately started in. "No, I never have. When your mother started seeing him and he started coming to the house, I didn't like how he looked at you."

"What? Eww, are you talking like sexually?"

"Of course not, you're Gramps would have castrated him." Gran waved her hand through the air. "No, he looked *at* you, but it was like he *didn't* see you. He'd listen when you talked, but it was as if it was taking up his time."

"Like he had to, instead of wanted to," I answered because I'd felt his indifference to me. It got to the point that the more he tried, the more he had creeped me out. He didn't want me around but put up with me for my mom's benefit.

"Exactly. Your mother and I argued when she told me Jacob got a better job and ya'll were moving. You'd already mentioned you didn't want to go, but she was adamant you move with them. She only let you stay when I brought to her attention that your Gramps and I wouldn't be close by to watch you when they wanted to go out or when Jacob took her with him on some of his trips." She shrugged when I stared at her. "The man is an asshole, always has been, and your mother has always been selfish. Not like I didn't tell her before she married him that I didn't like him. She chose to go through with the marriage, so dealing with him is on her, not the rest of us."

"I love you, Gran."

"The feeling is mutual, though I think I love you more."

"You know when the doctor came into the room and informed me that I was pregnant, my first thought was I needed to call Reed. Mom was the one to convince me to wait and think about it for a while. She'd told me if he had cared so much for me, he would have dealt with me leaving to help her. I argued with her and told her me leaving was suddenly dropped on him and though he brought up about long distance... You know what, it doesn't matter. In the end, it was my choice. Maybe I'm more like Mom than I thought, Gran. I never knew my dad, and I've done the same thing to my son. I'm going to have to accept that." I stood. "I need to check on Ry, and I'm praying I can reverse any damage I've caused him. I'll warm his food and take it with me, he needs to eat." I placed the food in the microwave while I rinsed my glass out and put it in the dishwasher.

"You're not like your mother, Raven."

"I'm not so sure about that. She got pregnant with me at seventeen and never told the man."

"Because, sweetheart, she didn't even know anything about him. She was waitressing part-time after school, and he'd stopped in for dinner while he was traveling through. I'd like to think the man didn't know her age, but with your mother, she probably didn't bother to tell him. She was wild growing up. Promiscuous. The more your gramps and I came down on her, the wilder she became. You were the opposite of her. She was always going somewhere; party, out with friends. You were a homebody from the day you were born. You'd cry the entire time when we'd take you out with us to shop, then quiet down as soon as we walked back in the house with you. As you got older and made friends, you never wanted to have sleepovers unless the girls came to our house." Gran smiled at me.

"What must have gone through your and Gramps mind when Reed started coming around?"

Gran chuckled. "Well…I can't say we weren't a little more than worried. We knew he was the son of the president of Haven MC. Knew the type of club it was then. But we also knew what could happen if we pressured you to stay away from him. We'd been through it with your mother. And to be honest, we figured he was your first boyfriend, and it would more than likely not last long. It did surprise us when it did, though. But by then, Reed had surprised us, too. He showed your gramps and I respect from day one. More importantly, he treated you with respect."

"The young good girl and the older bad boy. Really, Gran? That's a little cliché, don't you think?"

"You know, next time you get exasperated with Ry when he says something sarcastic or snarky—look in the mirror and you'll find who he gets that from." No matter

58

what type of mood I was in, Gran always could make me smile. "Now go and take care of Ry. I'll keep Reagan occupied, so she doesn't disturb the two of you."

"Thanks, Gran." After snagging a soda from the fridge and Ry's food, I headed out of the kitchen.

"Raven?"

I stopped in the doorway and looked over my shoulder. "Yes, Gran."

"It will all work out."

I gave a half smile. "Well, one can hope. But it can't get any worse, so there is that." I started walking toward the stairs, and with each step, I prayed I was right.

CM Books, LLC

Chapter Five

Keg

Wild Bill had no sooner said that we'd wait for Hawk when the knock at the door came. After he yelled open, the door cracked enough for Hawk's head to pop in. "We good in here?"

"Yeah," Prez responded. "We were waiting for you."

Hawk pushed the door the rest of the way open, then stepped back and Charlie walked in ahead of him. She was followed by Wyan, who was hired to work with her and the Matherson brothers after they picked him up for skipping out on bail the Matherson Brothers' Bail Bond side business had put up for him. The Mathersons had ties with the big man that went back to grade school, so when they'd gotten him out of trouble with the courts, they took him under their wings. Wyan's size, along with his good nature, made him prey for people. It didn't help he was a little slow mentally.

I stood to offer my chair to Charlie and gaped when I got a good look at her. Her clothes and hair were in disarray.

From the looks of her hair, it looked like a tornado touched down on her head and dislodged strands from her ponytail. But her jacket was what grabbed my attention, specifically the tear down one sleeve, which resembled a knife slash.

"What the hell happened to you?" I voiced.

"And whose ass do we need to hunt down?" Moose followed up with.

"Just a little mishap on a job," Charlie answered and took the seat I vacated.

I moved to the table and pulled a chair out, flipping it around before straddling it. I noticed Wyan shaking his head as he walked over and took a seat on the couch that rested against the opposite wall.

"Mishap my ass," Hawk replied as he did the same with the chair beside me, then sat.

From the glare Charlie shot in his direction, I could only guess they'd already argued over the incident.

"Don't start again with the macho crap. It's my job to chase bail runners."

Wyan snickered, and Hawk's head jerked in his direction. "Don't encourage her, Wyan. And where were you while she was rolling on the ground with the knife wielding bitch?"

"I was—" Willie didn't get to finish because Charlie used her hand as the universal stop sign while her eyes narrowed at Hawk.

"Oh no, you don't, mister. You've interfered enough with my job. You think I don't know you talked with Travis and that's why I have a shadow with me." Charlie threw her arm and used her thump to point in Wyan's direction.

"Whoa!" Moose yelled, and everyone's attention turned toward him. "Can we back up to her rolling around on the ground with another woman?"

"I don't know how sweet Katie puts up with you," Prez said and rubbed his eyes before pinching the bridge of his nose with his finger and thumb. When he rested his arms back on his desk, he looked at Charlie. "You wanna explain to us what happened so we can get down to business?"

"Sure thing. It's not much information, but I thought the club might be interested in it since the Widows are involved. The job I mentioned? I was following a tip on my drug dealer's whereabouts. He didn't show at court, and we've been tracking him for a week. Smalltime dealer who looks like he uses more of the product than he sells, but anyway, he was spotted at the Twilight Inn. You know the dump of a motel that's home to a few hookers and cheap enough that a few druggies can live off the streets and still have cash for the drug of their choice. Which in my book, it might be cleaner to shoot up in one of the empty buildings than one of the rooms at the Twilight."

"Charlie!" Hawk called out.

"What?"

"Can you get back on track and skip your evaluation of some of the places that our local law enforcement won't go near unless they enter as a group?"

My lips twitched, but I knew better than to laugh when Charlie rolled her eyes at Hawk's sarcastic comment.

"Whatever. So, my shadow and I hit the place, and as we are right at the door where the sleaze is supposed to be, it opens and he walks out. I reach for him with one hand while I grab for my handcuffs. That's when this bitch charges out of the room brandishing a knife. I moved but not enough, and the blade caught my jacket sleeve and sliced it. I let go of my bail jumper and knocked the knife out of her hand. Dumbass bitch decides she didn't need the knife and charges me. I go down, she goes down, and the wrestling starts. While I'm punching, she's pulling hair. Can't stand that shit. It pisses me off. Pulling hair and slapping. Please, you want to act like you're a badass, then throw a punch. Which I did, and it landed right on her chin. Snapped her head back and she was out. But my stoner used the distraction and bolted. When I looked around after the bitch was down, I see Wyan kneeling on the ground with one knee in the middle of the idiot's back.

"I call the cops to pick up the chick after I zip tie her, and while we wait for them, I go to where Wyan has my drugged-up runner pinned. He's begging Wyan not to let the cops go inside the room. I mean, it's not unusual when you're about to haul assholes back to jail that they threaten you. His crying, though, was new for me. So in between sniffles, he's mumbling about how he is going to be in serious trouble when the Widows find out about him being picked up, but with their product getting confiscated, he was a dead man."

"It isn't news the Widows are dealing drugs." Prez frowned, then asked Charlie, "Did you check out the room?"

CM Books, LLC

"I went back to the open door and looked in, and other than being dirty and cluttered with takeout containers, nothing stood out. Bounty hunter status doesn't allow us to do searches. Besides, I didn't want to disrupt anything in the room if the runner's babble held any truth." Charlie shrugged. "I called in and let Travis and the others know I retrieved our guy and filled them in on everything else, then waited for the cops. Didn't take long for them to arrive. I answered their questions, filled them in on what my runner said, then I was done. They put an officer on the woman who had come to right before they arrived, and Wyan was pulling our guy up so we could transport him. The lead officer had cleared us to leave. He said they'd do a search of the room and, depending on what they found, they'd file new charges on my guy. He would be in jail already, so they weren't worried. As Wyan and I started walking toward the parking lot, shit went south. Shots were fired. In the next second, I'm pushed down with three hundred and fifty plus pounds laying on top of me. Cops are yelling. Wyan helps me up off the ground, and when I look at my guy, he isn't moving. He's lying on the ground with a hole in his neck and chest. In less than five minutes the parking lot at the motel looks like a police convention. That's when I hear a bike and turn to see Hawk pulling in." Charlie glared at Hawk when she stopped for a breath.

"You can be pissed all you want. Travis called me because my woman was attacked with a knife. You think I'm not going to show up after that? Then I get there and see half a dozen cruisers and a body on the ground with my ol' lady standing next to it. I'm expected to stay calm?"

"I expect you to trust me to do my job. I expect you to give me enough credit that if I'm injured, I will call and let you know. The knife didn't even touch my skin. And stop using that term for me, I'm not old."

"Damn, woman, you draw trouble like a magnet. And the bail skippers should be really scared if you are the one after them," I said and received an elbow to my ribs from Hawk. "Come on, VP, you have to see it."

"Shut up, Reed. I do not draw trouble. It's always a possibility in my line of work. And the bail skippers are scared, they don't want caught," Charlie huffed.

"Uh…no. Not what I meant. Today your guy is shot dead, and what? Just two weeks ago the one you were after lands in the hospital with multiple breaks and a concussion from getting hit by a car. Admit it, dangerous shit happens around you." I chuckled when Charlie glared at me.

"Fuck off, it wasn't my fault the skipper ran into traffic while trying to outrun me. And today, the idiot's association with the Widows is what got his ass shot dead." Charlie crossed her arms over her chest.

"What about the guy last month? The one hit with the spilling paint from the scaffold on that apartment building when we were walking him past. My grandma washed my clothes three times to get the splatters of paint off." The office filled with male laughter at Wyan's words. His tale more than proved my point.

"Alright, settle down," Prez said, and I looked in his direction in time to catch him wiping at his eyes. Hell, I'd laughed so hard at Charlie's expense, my own eyes were leaking.

The laughter faded and the room went quiet as we tried to pull ourselves together. With no one talking, the knock on the door sounded extra loud in the room.

"Yeah!" Prez yelled.

When Roach acknowledged it was him, Charlie groaned. "You've got to be fucking kidding me. This club is worse than a bunch of gossiping old ladies! I'm going to taser whoever called him." I snorted when she aimed the last sentence at Hawk.

Charlie moved to the area in search of the grandfather she'd never met. And Roach never knew he had fathered a son or that he had a granddaughter until they'd crossed paths. So, Roach interrupting a meeting meant he knew Charlie was there and more than likely about what had happened earlier to her.

Prez told him to enter, and the door opened. Roach walked in and headed straight for Charlie.

"I'm fine," Charlie said and stood as he approached.

"I'll determine that for myself, missy." Roach started looking her up and down at that point, and Charlie looked as if she was going to pop a vein.

"So much for this meeting rapping up," Moose said and earned a glare from Hawk.

"Can we not have anyone else arguing? Charlie, why don't you go with Roach. Appreciate you taking the time to come in with Hawk." Prez leaned forward and added in a softer voice, "I know you didn't get to finish telling us everything, but Hawk can catch us up. Go spend a few minutes with your grandad. He looks like he needs it."

At my dad's words, Charlie's face softened and she nodded. "Come on, Wyan, let's go with Roach to the kitchen and see if we can find something to eat. We missed lunch." Charlie put her arm around Roach's waist, and we watched as they headed out of the office with Wyan behind them.

When the door clicked shut, Prez sat up straighter in his chair. "What everyone experienced is an example of why we don't let women attend meetings."

"Yes, it is. And thanks, Prez, for letting Charlie break the rule and come in and talk. I could have informed everyone, but she needed this. It gave her a chance to uncoil after the shit that happened this morning. She's tough and can handle her job. Better than I deal with her doing it. Her job could be the thing that kills me. Especially if I ever have to pull up on another scene like today." I slapped Hawk's back as he rubbed his hand over his neck.

I snorted. "I'd be more worried about her killing you. You're the one who told Roach, aren't you?"

"Texted him while I waited for her and Wyan to get out of the car when we got here. Said I brought Charlie here after she'd been on a job where a knife was pulled on her, and her skip was shot dead." I stared at Hawk, and he shrugged. "Figured I was already on her shit list for showing up after Travis called me. And before anyone asks, I have no remorse for throwing a brother under the bus."

CM Books, LLC

"Jesus Christ, Hawk. Maybe you better tell us the rest while you're still breathing. Roach figures out you set him up, he may kill you himself." Prez leaned back in his chair and shook his head.

"I'll take my chances. So, while I waited for Charlie to finish talking with the cops, Chief Knox pulled in. I walked over to talk to him as he got out of his cruiser. The bitch Charlie fought with. She belongs to one of the Widows. Her skip was more than likely there picking up supplies to sell. The room he was at was the chick's place. Chief said they've been hearing rumors that the Widows are stepping up their drug dealing, trying to bring it to a new level. PD knows they have to have a place to hide it, and they've been keeping an eye on them. New places they are spotted in, new people hanging around them or vice versus. They've come up with nothing. Widows have also recently gone away like the wind, which could be nothing more than lying low if they caught the cops sniffing around. Knox figures today was either already planned to get rid of the skip because who knows why, or the Widows have eyes on the girl and saw him get picked up and weren't happy with the prospect of losing their product. Took the skip out hoping it would take priority, and just maybe the cops would forget about searching the room. Chief believes it is the latter."

"Did he know if they found any drugs?" Prez asked.

"Yeah, the officer inside called it in, and the Chief was on his way before the shooting took place. They found a brick of coke hidden in the mattress. And while he was en route, they radioed again that they found packets of heroin, weed bags, and about ten grand in cash. It was hidden inside the door of the mini-fridge. The officer noticed when he opened the fridge the door looked like it had been tampered with, so he popped off the shelving part and surprise."

"Is this why you called the meeting, Prez? What do the Widows have to do with us other than being a wart on the club's ass from time to time?" I asked.

"It could be nothing with them other than them trying to expand. We need to keep an eye on them. The Widows have always been smalltime, so why now and how are they getting huge amounts of drugs into the area without us hearing a word? But they aren't the reason I called a meeting. Received a call first thing this morning from the FBI."

"Tell me it didn't have anything to do with Paul."

"No, Moose. Everything is good with Paul."

"Thank fuck. I'm not sure Katie could take anything else involving her dad."

"Nah, that's all good. They called to let us know Kosnoff died. Evidently, they had his mental ability checked after they took him into custody. Skipping the medical terms the therapist used as his diagnosis, it amounted to he is or was, considering he's dead, bat shit crazy."

"Prez, the man busted into an MC's clubhouse with the place full of brothers. With a six-shooter as his backup. Hell, that screams crazy in big, bold letters. The Feds actually needed a psychiatrist to clarify that?" I chuckled at my own statement. There's following procedure, then there's a waste of money. But I guess it all went hand-in-hand when dealing with anything the government was involved in.

70

"How the hell did he die?" Pinch asked, speaking for the first time since the meeting started. He, Crank, and Tram had been quiet since Charlie entered.

"Had a heart attack during the night. There'll be an autopsy to confirm it, but the medical examiner is confident he's right. No other signs, which translates into they don't think someone got to him."

Wasn't sure how the others felt, but I didn't care how the bastard died. He trafficked women, to me, the end result was what counted. Though, he did get off easy.

"Feds give you any updates on the others?" Tram asked.

Wild Bill's lip curled, and his eyes held a gleam. I knew that look on my dad's face, and I'm sure the others were just as intuitive. We've never doubted the trust in us, but as president, some things he wouldn't share. My brothers and I were okay with that because trust and loyalty went both ways, and it was the prez's way of protecting us.

Accountability: what you don't know can't come back and bite you in the ass.

"Only said the others were awaiting trial. Feds have a solid case against them. Stone and his little posse will soon be the newest residents of one or two of the Feds' luxury prisons. However, back to Kosnoff. When they were interrogating him about his network for trafficking, he kept telling them that they'd never shut it down. Then he'd giggled like he had a secret. He was already starting to lose his grip on reality, so the Feds aren't reading too much into it. They're confident they got his networking shut down."

71

"Then what's their issue?" Hawk asked.

"Two women, from two different cities close to the border, went missing within two weeks of each other. They're looking into the incidents because one girl's family is putting a lot of pressure on them. Dad's some bigwig and he's certain his daughter was taken. The agent didn't go into it. He was just told to give us a heads up. If it's someone trying to take over with Kosnoff out of the picture, the Feds may need our services at some point. They want to clip the wings before any new organization takes off. But they also said was everything they've looked at for the two cases screams runaway or daughter running off with a boyfriend." Prez blew out a breath. "That wraps shit up, at least for today. Anyone got anything to ask or add before the meeting ends?"

I looked around at the others and like me were shaking their heads no, all except Crank. He leaned over and rested his arms on his legs with his hands dangling between them. His expression one of a person wrapped in thought.

"This shit from the Feds on the two women, how sure are they it isn't Kosnoff related. Hell, with the Widows' new business plan—do you think it could the Widows expanding their business of drugs to trying their hands at trafficking?" Crank had a solid question. I wouldn't discount the Widows, but they didn't have the members to execute both sides.

"I'm not going to disregard anything, Crank. If the Widows were larger in numbers, they'd be the first ones to look in to. Like I said before, let's keep our eyes on the Widows and ears open for any info on new players in the

72

area. Might have this club running legit now, but it's still our territory. Now, meeting over." Prez slapped his hand down on the desk, and my brothers and I stood.

"I'm going to check on Charlie. Make sure Roach is still alive. Then I'll be ready to help you move shit to your new place." Hawk slapped my back.

I snorted. "Hell, Charlie's right. We do gossip like a bunch of old women." The others laughed.

"Do not tell that woman she is right. I won't be able to live with her." Hawk did a fake shiver. I shook my head. Between Charlie and Hawk, I wasn't sure who liked arguing more, it seemed to be a form of foreplay for the two of them.

"Thanks, I'd appreciate the help. Came to the club to gather some help after I dropped the bomb about buying a house. The meeting and the shit show earlier kinda pushed that plan aside," I said and started for the door with the others behind me. "Won't take long to move my things. That is what's great about an apartment, you don't collect a bunch of crap."

"No, because most of your crap is in my shed." My dad laughed and swung his arm over my shoulder. "Maybe now you can get all of your shit out of there."

I laughed. "I hear ya. I'll come over soon and go through the stuff. Pitch what I don't want and then take the other stuff to my place. The house has a decent size shed in the back."

We reached the end of the hallway, and Hawk turned toward the kitchen while the rest of us headed for the door

73

leading outside. While we waited on Hawk, we discussed how best to get the job done.

When Hawk walked outside, he was followed by Smoke and Fire. "Rounded up two more and texted Latch to bring a truck."

"Appreciate it. Food and beer on me."

"That's a given. Why do you think we're helping?" Pinch said as he walked to his bike.

"No, shit. Hope he doesn't think it's because we like him," Crank joked, then mounted his bike.

As I prepared to get on my bike, Moose stepped up to his motorcycle parked beside mine. Before he kicked the bike over, he looked at me. "We give you shit because you're the youngest out of us, but all joking aside, I hope you know each one of us has your back. Whether it's helping you move or giving you support on the kid front."

Moose didn't wait for me to reply, he fired up his bike and pulled out behind my dad. Bringing up the rear, riding with my brothers, it was the best feeling in the world.

It would take time getting to know my son, but I couldn't wait to share this experience with him like my dad had done with me.

Chapter Six

Raven

"Yeah," was Ry's reply after I knocked on the bedroom door.

Luckily my grandparents had a four bedroom home, so Ry and Reagan could each have their own room while we looked for a place of our own. I was occupying the same bedroom I always did when at my grandparents' house. Whether living there or visiting.

"Can I come in? I brought food with me."

"Sure." I wasted no time opening his door because I didn't want to chance he'd change his mind.

Ry sat on the bed with his back up against the headboard, twirling one of many motorcycle models he'd put together. He had a shelf in his room at our home in North Carolina and the different models lined up on it followed the age he'd been when he'd put it together. His skill level increased with each one.

CM Books, LLC

I walked to the bed and set the tray down on the nightstand. Then I sat on the edge of the bed next to him. "You did a great job with that one." I pointed to the model, it was the last one he'd put together and the only one he'd kept with him, instead of packing it away in storage with the others.

"Thanks."

"You should eat before it gets cold."

"Not hungry right now."

"Okay. How about you pick what we have for dinner?"

"I don't care. Reagan can pick."

Not once in the exchange did Ry lift his eyes to mine. He kept them on the model as he turned it over and over.

"You want to talk about what happen today, Ry?"

The silence was worse than the short replies. I would have paid any amount of money to know what he was thinking. It seemed like hours passed by while I waited, but when I looked over at the clock on his table, it had only been twenty minutes.

When Ry finally looked at me, his expression was unreadable. "Do you think I love motorcycles because of him?"

"Well, I'm not sure it falls under traits that are passed down to children, but you never know."

"He was really cool and nice when he talked to me before he got mad and was yelling at you."

"He was angry with me. So were you, Ry. You shut down, where Reed was vocal with his anger. You'll have to make your own decision about Reed, Ry. *I can tell you* what type of person he is, but it isn't a guarantee *you'll see* him that way. To be honest, he could have changed. I doubt it, but today was the first contact with him I've had since he was nineteen, and I was a couple months shy of seventeen. I wish I could tell you how to feel about him, but I can't. All I can say is give him a chance. You both had a bomb dropped on you today, huh?"

"My middle name is after him, isn't it?"

"Yes. When you were born, I named you Ryker Reed Newhouse. Then your last name changed to Allen once your dad and I were married."

"Mom?"

"What is it, Ry? You can ask me anything."

"Did Da...Derek know about him?"

"Yes, and Derek may not have been biologically your dad, but he loved you as if he was. It's okay to still refer to him as your dad. You understand?"

"Then what do I call *him*?"

"Oh, sweetie, it's up to you. I'm not in a position to tell either you or Reed how to deal with this. I'm the cause of it. My decisions, right or wrong, have done enough damage to the both of you. I'll be here, but it will be up to you and him on where you go."

"Why did you do it?" And there was the question I waited for.

"I could blame everything on being seventeen years old and leave it at that, but you deserve so much more from me. How about I start at the beginning? When I'm done, if you have more questions, I'll answer them the best I can."

I took Ry's nod as a go-ahead. Taking a deep breath and letting it out, I began to explain. Not sure exactly where to start. There aren't many teenage boys who'd want to hear how their young parents fell in love, and it wasn't enough. And Reed and I were in love, it was why it hurt so much when it ended.

"You know a little. Like I moved in with Gran and Gramps when Nana and Pappy Jacob moved to Raleigh. And then, I moved in with Nana after her car accident. Reed and I had dated before I moved, and since I didn't know if I would be back or even when, we ended our relationship. After a few months with Nana, I found out I was pregnant with you. I was torn on telling Reed because of the breakup. I wasn't sure how he would take the news. I was young, Ry. It isn't an excuse, but when you're young, you look at things differently and make decisions that you probably wouldn't if you were older. If I were in the same situation now, I would pick the phone up and call Reed. Leaving the decision his if he wanted to be part of the baby's life. Instead, I kept him out of the equation without considering his feelings. Sometimes, though, I would look at you and question my choice. But in my mind, time had passed by and I felt it was too late. Using that as an excuse when, in truth, I was scared to face Reed. Not because I was afraid of what he would do, it was because I didn't want him to hate me. It amounts to being selfish.

"You weren't even three when Derek came into our lives. You took to him immediately, and it scared me. I started wondering if I cheated you out of a father/son bond, which again, had me questioning not telling Reed about you. And your dad…Derek fell hard for you, too. I won't say it made it easier on me, it did make me feel that maybe I had made the right decision. Then when he asked me to marry him, he also asked to become your dad, legally, not just because of the marriage. He wanted you to share his name, too. I agreed, and he was listed on your birth certificate. You were four.

"I finished college and then went straight into veterinarian medicine. Looking back, I'm not sure how we juggled it all: young, married, both of us still in school… We even added Reagan to the family before graduating from NCSU College of Veterinary Medicine. But we did it all.

"Looking back at how busy we were with everything, at some point, I stopped worrying. You were getting older, and by then, it didn't seem as important. You were happy, Derek loved you, and you loved him, and I guess a part of me didn't want to be the reason for it all to crash around you. As your parent, it's my job to protect you, and in doing so, I'm the one that's caused you the most pain. I can't go back and change it, but I promise I'll help you adjust in any way you need me to," I finished and waited for Ry to absorb everything I told him.

"If we hadn't moved here, would you have ever told me about my real dad?"

CM Books, LLC

Grownups underestimate how much a child comprehends.

"I'm not sure, Ry. I'd like to think I would have eventually because in my heart I knew it was wrong not to. Once the decision to move back was made, I also knew at some point, I'd have to come clean. There'd be no way of avoiding Reed forever, and it would be only a matter time that we ran into him. Him seeing you, your looks, your age… He'd realize the timing fit. So, I was prepared to tell him and you, I was just trying to grow the courage."

"I overheard you and Nana arguing."

I frowned. "What?"

"You and Nana were in the kitchen, and I was coming from my room. I heard you discussing us moving here. She tried talking you out of it. I thought it was because she'd miss us being so far away. Then she said that you'd be a fool to think the truth would stay buried if you moved back. I didn't understand what she meant."

I thought back and tried to remember the conversation. It was after Gramps had called about wanting to retire. To me, it was perfect timing, the kids and I needed a change. The decision to take over his practice and move back to Washington was made during the call. My mother showed up shortly after, and I'd caught her by surprise telling her of my decision. I told her it was for the best. It would be the final step in healing from the loss of Derek. A clean slate for the three of us to form a life without him, leaving the constant memory of him every time we walked into the house. We'd argued, and Ry was right with what he'd overheard. She and I had dropped the subject when he walked into the kitchen. It never crossed my mind he'd heard any of the argument.

"She was talking about my real dad finding out, wasn't she?"

Yeah, adults didn't give kids enough credit.

"Yes." What else could I have said? He'd deserved the truth from me.

He ran his hand over the model, then set it on the nightstand by his uneaten food. "I'm hungry now."

I glanced at the hamburger and fries that had surely gone cold. "I think we deserve homemade pizza after today. What do you think?" I stood. "It's probably about time for Gramps to get home. Why don't you come downstairs and help me make the pizza?"

"Sure." Ry got off the bed, and we started walking toward the door. "I love you, Mom."

"I love you, too, Ry. So much." A huge weight was lifted, and I knew no matter how everything else played out from here, I wouldn't lose my son.

I pulled the last pizza from the oven just as Gramps walked in the door from the garage with Sabith, his fifteen-year-old German Sheppard, trotting beside him. Since I could remember, he'd always taken his dogs to work with him. When Sage, the GS he'd had when I was little, passed away, he'd went a while before getting another dog. Then one day, he walked in with six-month-old Sabith. Gramps was on a call at the shelter when her owners brought her in.

81

They surrendered her to the shelter because they were moving and the place they were going to be renting didn't allow for pets. I don't think I'll ever understand why people get animals, then so easily discard them.

"Smells and looks as if I have perfect timing."

"Yes, you do. How was the rest of the day? Sorry, I didn't make it back in."

Gramps looked toward the living room, then back at me. "I heard you had a good reason."

"Maybe, but that left you shorthanded. Yesterday I saw the schedule for today. A lot of afternoon appointments."

"Well, Candice ended up having to call and rescheduled most of them. A couple clients couldn't be reached, but they waited until I came back."

"Where did you have to go?"

"I sent you on the call to Haven because I needed to go to the shelter. They had a dog brought in that was in bad shape and more than they could handle. I stabilized the poor thing, then brought her to the clinic. After dinner, I'm going back to stay so I can keep a close eye on her. Not sure she's going to make it through the night." Gramps' clinic served as the on-call vet for the local animal shelter.

"What happened to her?" Listening to Gramps made me feel worse about not going into the clinic. But Ry had needed me more. At least I could set aside the inkling that Gramps sent me to Haven on the house call to give me a push toward telling Reed.

82

"Not sure. Shelter said the man who dropped her off had picked her up off the side of the road. Not too far from here. He'd seen her and stopped not even sure she was alive until he noticed her chest lift when he'd gotten closer. He wrapped her in a tarp he had in his truck and drove her to the shelter. She was emaciated, so guessing she was a stray and by her wounds, she'd been in a fight recently with either another dog or a coyote."

"Aw, poor thing. I hope she makes it."

"If I can get her through the next twenty-four hours, she just might," he said as he poured Sabith's food in her bowl. "How about you, pumpkin? You and Ry going to be okay?"

"Yeah, I think so. I talked with Ry and he's handling it pretty well. As for me, it went as well as I had expected."

Gramps lowered his voice, "And, Reed, after the initial explosion?"

"The timing may have been off, but once he cooled down a bit, he seemed…resigned. Guess I'll really know after tomorrow. He's coming here for answers."

"I know it might seem bad right now, but I think when the dust settles, it will be a good thing."

"You always did like Reed."

"I don't know if I'd go that far." He smiled, and I laughed.

Gran and the kids walked into the kitchen, and we sat down to eat. Ry and Reagan seemed no worse for wear as we ate. As usual the conversation around the table was about the dog Gramps was taking care of. Reagan had a huge heart when it came to animals and wanted to go back to the clinic with him. She got a tad upset when she was told she couldn't, but there was no way she needed to be there if the dog didn't make it.

I wondered how long it would take for the elephant in the room to be exposed. And I should have anticipated Reagan would be the one to yank the cover off.

"Ry has another daddy," she blurted, and I could have sworn Gramps's lips twitched before he got it under control.

"You don't say," Gramps said as he looked at Ry.

I held my breath as I waited to see if or how Ry answered. But with a million guesses, it wasn't something I would have ever expected him to say.

"Yeah. At least now, I know why I'm not as crazy about animals like the rest of the family. I like motorcycles like Reed."

I looked at Gran and she smiled with a look that said, *I told you it would be okay.*

"Well, that's pretty cool, huh?" Gramps asked.

"Uh huh, I guess. Now maybe Mom will let me have a dirt bike. It's in my blood."

"Then, I get a dog. It's in my blood," Reagan replied.

And like that, our little part of the world was back to normal. Thank God for the resilience of children. They could teach adults a lot about handling the bumps life places in the road.

Chapter Seven

Keg

Making my way from the bedroom to the kitchen and finding the coffee pot ready just waiting for me to push the button was definitely something I could get used to. Thanks to my brothers' ol' ladies who showed up while we were moving my stuff.

The move from my apartment to the house was done in a few hours, and though I was thankful for the help from my brothers, we were men, not decorators. Informed of that fact by the ol' ladies when Pinch and Crank dropped the couch in the wrong spot.

Between Katie, Charlie, Macy, and Tink, my boxes were unpacked, the kitchen was put together—and my brothers and I schooled on the importance of the furniture being placed correctly to bring a room together. I laughed, and so did the others only to receive glares that would've silenced the most seasoned badass.

The women hadn't seemed to care that my household possessions consisted of a bedroom set, a couch, two tables, a recliner, a couple lamps, and basic kitchen items that allowed me to cook a meal. Clothes and personal items finished off the boxes we'd toted into the house. The most expensive items in my belongings, a seventy-two-inch television, a surround sound system, and the gaming console to keep me entertained when alone.

When the women made a list of items I needed now—not when I got around to buying them—I gladly pulled out my credit card and handed it over with, "Grab whatever you think I need."

My dad walked by carrying a box and shook his head as Charlie snatched the card from my hand. And Moose, Hawk, Smoke, and Fire laughed when the women left chattering about what they would do with my house if it were theirs.

When I asked my brothers, "What the hell is so funny?" They'd laughed harder.

"So much for having a brother's back. The bastards had known," I said out loud as I looked down at the receipt on the counter and wondered how four women could do that much damage to a man's bank account in two hours. Then, I turned my head toward the living room where throw pillows laid on my couch, positioned just so. They were only a few of the many items the women had returned with. My bed had new sheets, the bathroom off my bedroom and the half bath in the hall now had matching rugs and towels.

CM Books, LLC

Reaching for a coffee cup in the cabinet beside the sink, because all dishes and glasses needed to be close to the dishwasher that was underneath the counter right below said cabinet. Pulling open the drawer next to the dishwasher to grab a spoon, I rolled my eyes.

Who the fuck cares about a utensil holder thing? But I had one.

"That was a pricey lesson," I said out loud and grabbed my coffee and headed to my bedroom. I needed to get cleaned up. Answers waited for me.

Showered and dressed, I walked out of the bedroom to the sound of my cell ringing. I'd left it on the kitchen bar and hurried to grab it. Not taking the time to look at who was calling, I swiped the screen.

"Keg," I said as I answered.

"I hope so since it was your number I dialed."

"Am I supposed to know you?" I grinned in preparation for the reply.

"Don't be an ass, jerk face."

"Oh, I know who you are now. The FedEx man's kid."

"You know the reason Mom and Dad had me? Because they couldn't accept anything less than perfection." I groaned, and Sami's laughter boomed in my ear.

"How long have you been holding onto that one, sis?"

"They just come to me. What can I say?"

"Yeah, 'cause you are funny. Funny looking anyway."

"Alright, I'm done. Now tell me about my nephew, Reed."

I laughed. "Well, I see you've talked to our dad already this morning."

"Yeah, yeah. I know you bought a house, and I want to hear all about it, but not right now. Get to the kid."

"Speaking of kids. How's Ally doing?"

"Same, causing trouble. Now quit stalling."

Humor gone, I leaned against the counter. "I have a son named Ry with a woman that if you told me two days ago she was capable of keeping this type of information from me, I would have called you a liar. Damn it, Sami. He's twelve."

"Dad said you're going to her grandparents' house today."

"Yeah. I couldn't deal with Raven anymore yesterday. I lost my temper, scared her and her little girl. Some first impression on my kid, huh?"

There was enough of a pause that I held the phone out to see if we were still connected before putting it back to my ear.

"You need to hear Raven out, Reed. Let her explain. Don't forget I've been in her shoes."

Shit, I'd forgotten it hadn't been that long ago that Speed found out about Ally.

"Speed left, Sami. You went to tell him and he was gone. I've been right here."

"You've always been on my side and taken up for me. Yes, when I found out I was pregnant, I went to the Black

Hawk's compound, but I took the easy out and took Kane being gone as an excuse. Instead of turning and walking away that day, I should've spoken to the president and told him. They knew where Kane was. I can't even use the excuse that I didn't know how MCs worked."

"Okay, I'll give you similar situations. But, Sami, another man is raising my kid as his own. Raven allowed it. I want to have a relationship with my son, I'm just not sure how. And that is only part of it. I mean, I know I have to build a relationship with him, but I'm going to have to deal with Raven. I'm not sure I'll ever forgive her."

"Reed, you changed after Raven left."

"I did not!"

"Oh, please. You loved her, she left, and you changed. You went from being devoted to one girl, which for a male raised in an MC is a feat in itself, to a male whore. Let's be honest, I'm surprised this is the only kid to surface that's yours."

"Is this supposed to be a helpful speech because it isn't."

"Don't go getting pissed. I'm not scared of your temper. Seriously, Reed, and I say this with all the sister love in me—get over yourself. It isn't that your feelings aren't important, they are, but there is someone else involved in this that deserves to come first, the boy. Hear Raven out and give her a chance to explain. You loved her once. And you might find it easier than you think to forgive her. As far as Ry, just be yourself. The two of you will work it out. You've

CM Books, LLC

got a good heart, Reed. Ry will see that, too. And if you tell anyone I said that, I'll have to hurt you."

"Thanks, sis."

"Anytime. Call if you need me. I'm not that far away. I'll always have your back, Reed."

"I know, Sami."

"Hey, and if I'm wrong and Raven has turned into a raving bitch—let me know and I'll bring Carly with me so she can kick Raven's ass."

I chuckled. Carly grew up with Sami here at Haven. They were best friends and Carly spent a lot of time at our house to get away from her parents. She was Stone's daughter. At least then, that was what everyone thought, including Stone. When our dad, Wild Bill, president of Haven wanted Sami someplace safe while we did the final push to clean out the club, Carly was sent with her because Stone, her dad, was the reason for the cleanup. Wild Bill called on a few men who he served with in his time in the military. They just happened to be the officers of Black Hawk MC.

Sami ended up with Speed, one of the enforcers, and Carly, who vowed never to get tangled up into another club, ended up with Crusher, the current president of Black Hawk. He'd taken the reins when his dad stepped down. The biggest shock to come from what was supposed to be a temporary move wasn't Ally, Sami's daughter with Speed. It was that Carly found out she wasn't Stone's daughter after all. She was the daughter of one of the Black Hawk originals who was killed by Stone's treachery. Speed was Cutter's son, and when it was all said and done, Carly turned out to be Speed's sister. One thing was for sure, MC life was never boring.

I glanced at the time. "Going to let you go. I want to head to Raven's."

"Okay. Don't forget to keep that temper in check."

"I will. Love you, brat."

"Love you, too, jerk."

No sooner than I hung up with Sami, my cell rang again.

I swiped the screen, then answered, "Hey, Dad. I know you talked with Sami, she called already."

"Good, but that's not why I'm calling. Can you swing by the clubhouse before you head to Raven's?"

"Yeah, what's going on?"

"Freak's snake died overnight. He wants to bury it today."

"Okay, do I need to drop a box off for it or something?"

"No. You need to swing by because he wants to have a funeral."

"You're shitting, right?"

"I really wish I was. Just be there, Reed. I've still got to call Crank and Moose."

"I'll be there."

"See you in a few."

After I hung up with my dad and struggled with the fact I was going to the club because we were having a club burial for a snake, I grabbed my keys and walked out. My

91

phone vibrated as I waited in the driveway for the garage door to close. Pulling it out, I read the text.

Moose: *Do you think we should grab flowers?*

I didn't bother to reply. I shoved the cell into the pocket inside my vest and started down the driveway.

⚜

Every brother in the club stood in the woods behind the clubhouse and watched one of the oldest members of Haven, Freak, shed tears as his closest friend and club brother, Shock, shoveled the last of the dirt on the box containing his pet rattlesnake. Katie stood on one side of Freak while Charlie stood on the other, both women swiping at the tears in their eyes.

When Shock was finished, we walked back to the clubhouse. Freak in front led by Katie and Charlie.

"If other MCs get wind of this, they're going to demand our club patch," Tram said, his voice low so Freak wouldn't overhear.

"Fuck 'em. Besides, this was important to Freak, so that makes it important to us." Even if I thought the ritual was flat out nuts, I'd never do or say anything to hurt Freak's feelings. None of us would.

"You didn't answer my text." Moose moved beside me.

"No, because that was fucked up."

"Uh, it wasn't a joke. Katie asked me, and I had no damn clue. When you didn't answer, she made me stop at the flower shop on the way."

CM Books, LLC

"What made you choose daisies, Moose," Crank said from behind Moose and me.

Thank God we'd reached the clubhouse and everyone else had gone inside, leaving only me, Moose, Pinch, Tram, Hawk, Crank, Roach, and my dad.

"It was the only flowers I could remember when Katie made me go in while she took a call from the hospital. I sure as fuck wasn't going to ask the woman behind the counter what flowers would be best for a snake's funeral," Moose responded, and so much for keeping our composure as we laughed due to the ridiculousness of it all.

Roach sober up first. "You know this is probably going to send Freak into a case of depression. We need to keep an eye on him. He and Shock both have shown an enormous change with the additions of Katie and Charlie into the club."

"You're right, Roach. I don't want to see this set either one of them back. It's been nice having them join in more." My dad wasn't the only one enjoying the social changes in the two men.

"I'll let the prospects know to keep watch on them, too. They can switch off staying at the clubhouse at night."

"Good call, Hawk. Always someone around during the day," Pinch added.

"Well, if you don't need me to stick around, I'm going to head out to Raven's." I looked at my dad.

"Hold up a minute. I was going to call a meeting, but this won't take long."

"I'll head inside, Prez, and give you all some privacy," Roach said and turned toward the door.

"No need, Roach," Prez said, and Roach stopped where he was to listen. "When I got home yesterday from us helping Keg, I received a call from Chief Knox. He asked us to be backup for the department if they find out where the Widows have set up shop. I agreed to it, then double checked with General Patel to make sure we weren't on point for any mission with the government. We aren't slated right now. Filled him in on the Chief's and our thoughts about the Widows stepping up into bigger business and expanding their territory. General agreed the evidence points to it. I even brought up Crank's thought about the women with him. And if the Widows have anything to do with those two women being snatched, then the Chief is going to lose the lead on any case involving the Widows because the Feds will step in. They will then become our problem. For now, standby is our part. Eyes and ears open when you are out. This could turn out to be nothing, but what worries me if it's true. The Widows know we won't stand for it in our territory, so I could see them doing something to send us a message."

"Slimy fuckers."

"Yes, they are, Moose."

"Is that it? Standby until needed, but we keep watch?" I asked, making sure we were all on the same page.

"Yeah," Prez answered, then looked toward Hawk. "Check with the Matherson brothers. See if they know anything about the Widows. Since Wyan's working with the brothers now, maybe he's given them some info on the Widows we don't know. More information we gather, the better."

"You got it. The Widows have always been low-key, if they are making a push, I wonder if leadership has changed. T-bone Jones is their leader. At least he was. Might need to look into that, too. Could be they have a shift in power."

Hawk was right. Gangs were notorious for rolling over the top spot. Respect and loyalty were easily switched from one player to the next, depending on who was stronger and had more ambition. Probably why it crawled right up most MC's backs when they got referred to as gangs.

"Well, we have a start. Guess we should go in and check on Freak." Prez's words were our cue the impromptu meeting was over.

"I'm out of here. If you need me, text." Anxious to get to Raven's, I turned to leave. I planned to walk around the building, instead of cutting through the clubhouse.

"Hey!" I stopped when Moose yelled. "Same goes, brother. You need us, you call or text."

I gave a chin lift in response. I knew Moose spoke for each of them. They'd be there whether I needed them physically or just to talk. Their support meant everything to me.

CM Books, LLC

CM Books, LLC

Chapter Eight

Raven

With the first sounds of a motorcycle heading up the drive, I stepped out onto the front porch. I'd had butterflies flapping their wings in my stomach, anticipating Reed's arrival and nervous about the outcome.

It didn't escape me that I stood in the exact spot more times than could be counted. The difference was then it was the excitement of spending time with him.

He didn't look at me until he stopped, unsnapped his helmet and dismounted the bike. When he gave a small smile in my direction as he placed the helmet on his vacated seat, the gesture felt huge to me.

"I would have been here a little earlier, but I had to swing by the clubhouse for a bit." He walked to the bottom of the steps that led to the porch.

"Did you go to check on Frankie? He called early this morning to let me know Rattler died during the night."

"Freak called you, not one of the other brothers?"

The way he asked had me frowning. "Yes. Why wouldn't he? It was his pet after all."

"It's no big deal. He usually is…standoffish with new people. Just surprised me that he was the one to make the call."

"Oh." I'd never felt so awkward around Reed. I inhaled then exhaled. "We can talk inside if you want." I started to turn but realized he hadn't made a move to walk up the stairs.

"Where's Ry and Reagan?"

"Gran took them to Gramps' clinic. He stayed there last night to watch over a dog that was in a bad way. Being Saturday, the clinic's closed, so they went to help clean out the kennels and feed the other animals that are there. I thought it best they weren't here for my inquisition."

"Alright. Understandable. I just hope sending him off somewhere every time I come to see him doesn't become a habit."

I noticed he might have looked calm on the outside, but his words…the anger wasn't buried too deep.

"I won't keep you from seeing him, Reed." After I answered him, my words played back in my head, and I cringed.

"Why's today different or tomorrow? Is it because I found out about him, and you have no choice now?"

"You know what? Fuck you, Reed. I screwed up. I'm a lying, deceitful bitch for keeping him from you. I get that. Yet I stand here owning it. If you want the sordid details of my master plan, fine—if not, come see Ry anytime you like.

98

The house phone number is the same. If you don't remember it, look it up. It's listed under Herbert Newhouse. I do ask that you consider spending time with Ry here until he's more comfortable around you." The situation was of my doing, but I wasn't a doormat. I've lived and will continue to live with what the decision I made had cost him and Ry, that's on me. I just refused to let Reed continuously throw it in my face. I turned and reached for the door handle.

"Raven, wait."

I turned to face him.

"I'm sorry. That shit was uncalled for. It goes for yesterday, too. I should have handled it a little better."

"You were caught off guard, and then you got pissed. I understand, Reed. I really do. I expected no less when you found out. You may have trouble believing this, but I was planning to tell you. I knew I couldn't avoid you once I moved back permanently. Anyway, it's okay. Call when you want to see Ry, and while you're here, I'll stay out of your way. I'm working at the clinic most days, eight-thirty to five. Or later depending on patients."

"I'd still like to know why."

"Okay. Would you like to come in? Or we could sit out here."

"It's a nice day. Sitting out here would be good."

"I'll get us something to drink. Beer, tea, water?"

"Water is fine. Your husband going to join us?" My face must have had a weird expression when I looked at him because he added. "Earlier, you didn't mention he went with the kids, so I assume he's inside."

"Oh." I looked at my now bare left hand. How awkward was it going to be discussing Derek with Reed? The two men in my life that I've loved and lost. Maybe I was flawed and never meant for happiness. I steeled my spine and looked at Reed. "You noticed the band yesterday? I've been struggling with removing it. Removing seemed to be the last part connecting me to Derek. But this morning, I took it off and put it with my engagement ring. My husband, Derek, died in an ATV accident almost a year ago. He was out on a call for horse, and the farm used ATVs to get around, it was a large spread. He tended the horse and was riding back to the barn and he must not have seen the fallen branch. It was the only explanation for the accident to have happened. He hit it and the ATV went up on two wheels, he was thrown, and his head hit the ground first. The weight and momentum of his body… He broke his neck. Once he was picked up by the ambulance and taken to the hospital, I received the call he'd been injured. At the hospital, the doctor told me he died instantly. Honestly, I didn't hear all the medical terms after they told me he was dead."

I wiped the few tears that slipped from the corners of my eyes. A few were an improvement over the sobbing that followed any mention of Derek's death for a month after it happened. Mine and the kids' lives changed in a blink of an eye.

"Christ, Raven." Reed was up the stairs and had his arms around me before he finished talking.

The comfort he offered me even with what I had done to him, I shared my thoughts. "I lost you and then him.

I'm unsure if I could handle losing anything else." I placed my arms around his waist and absorbed the warmth being in Reed's arm provided. Then I cried in earnest, but for the first time in a year, it wasn't because of Derek's death; it was because being in Reed's arms felt like coming home. And what did that say about me?

We stayed that way for a few minutes until I stepped back out of his arms and again wiped my tears away. "Let me get those drinks."

"We aren't going to have too many more nice days." He looked me up and down before he continued, "Grab a jacket and let's go for a ride. What do you say?"

Reed was looking at me and when I looked back at him, I didn't want to misread anything wrong out of his softened expression. Instead, I turned and opened the door. "I'll only be a minute."

I hurried to my room and grabbed my jacket, my key to the house and my phone. I put the phone in one of the jacket's pockets and shoved some cash in the front pocket of my jeans. In the kitchen, I left a note in case Gran and the kids were back before I was. Then on the way out of the kitchen I snagged a couple bottles of water.

When I stepped back outside, locking the door and pulling it shut behind me, Reed was standing beside his bike. As I approached, he held out a helmet to me and took the water bottles from me and placed them in the open saddlebag he must have pulled the helmet from.

"You care if we hit a drive-thru while we're out? I missed breakfast and lunch."

101

"I don't mind."

"You remember how to ride?" He grinned as he snapped his helmet in place.

"I think I can handle it." I smiled back as I snapped my own clasp.

"Well, we are about to see." He patted the top of my helmet, then straddled the bike and turned it over. Holding it up with both feet planted on the ground, he looked over his shoulder. "I think you've forgotten." His lips twitched. "You actually have to get on to ride, Rav."

"Smartass." Once I was on the back with my arms wrapped around his waist, he pulled out slowly. When we hit the main road and kicked up the speed, I tightened my hold and leaned into him.

God, I'd forgotten how good it felt.

I don't know how long we'd been riding before we'd pulled into a fast food drive-thru, and Reed ordered several burgers before pulling to the side in the parking lot, long enough to stash them in one of the saddlebags before taking off again. Frankly, I didn't care. I just knew I didn't want the relaxing, freeing feeling to go away. On the back of his bike, I didn't have to think about the talk to come, I could let the memories flow and take me temporarily back to another time. We'd been young, carefree, and the future held promise. It may not have been healthy for me to reflect on our past, but it was better than facing what laid ahead.

CM Books, LLC

The bike slowed, and the jarring of going from pavement to gravel had me taking in my surroundings. Reed parked and waited for me to get off the bike first.

"I always loved this park. I haven't had the chance to bring the kids here." I set my helmet on the seat once Reed had dismounted.

"We used to come here and just hang out and talk. Figured maybe it would work today, too."

"Sure," I agreed, though not certain if I'd be able to come back to this spot after today.

Collecting the burgers and the bottles of water, we walked side by side into the park, choosing one of the picnic tables that was off to the side and away from the other family taking advantage of the warm weather for a picnic.

The park wasn't anything elaborate—several tables surrounding a small playground for young children. It was perfect if you wanted a stress-free place to share a picnic and let your kids blow off a little steam.

Setting one of the burgers and a bottle of water in front of me, Reed then took a seat across the table and folded back the paper wrapping on his own burger. I unwrapped mine and pulled a small piece off, and popped it in my mouth. More for something to do than because I was hungry.

Reed demolished the first burger and balled up the wrapper, then pick up another burger.

"Sorry. Hungrier than I thought." He glanced down at my burger as I continued to pick at it. "I know you're nervous, Raven. Don't be. I need the reason, that's it. It will

103

help me understand where your head was. I know we can't go back, but understanding may make going forward easier. Regardless of the snide remarks I threw at you earlier, I don't want to keep doing that. I want to lay this to rest, move on and get to know Ry. I definitely don't want to waste time with what ifs."

He was right. I pushed the burger aside and reached for the water bottle. After twisting off the top and taking a drink, I looked Reed in the eye and stepped off the ledge.

"I didn't know I was pregnant when I left here. Even though we split up, I'm not sure I would have left if I'd known. Not even to help my mom. That day when you rode up, I was sad about having to tell you I was leaving, then you said there wasn't any sense in staying in touch, and a long distance relationship wasn't in the cards—it crushed me. I've had a lot of time to think about that day. Anyway…"

Reed never said a word as I recounted everything from the moment I found out I was pregnant, to my decision not to tell him for fear of his rejection of Ry, which would have crushed me all over again.

He sat quietly while I talked about meeting Derek and his acceptance of Ry. Even the day Derek was added as the father on Ry's birth certificate. Every detail laid out for his judgment.

I'm not sure when I moved my focus off him to the bottle in my hand. But at some point, I had because as I reached the ending and brought us to Haven the day he found out, there was a small puddle under the bottle from

104

the condensation I unknowingly helped slide down the bottle with my finger.

"That's it. You were present for the rest." When I looked back at him, his face was unreadable. Seconds ticked by as I waited for a response from him. I wouldn't rush him. I'd sit there as long as it took.

"It sounds like you thought often about getting in touch with me. Yet continued to choose to keep Ry a secret."

I wasn't sure he was expecting me to respond or processing all that I shared. So I remained quiet. Since he hadn't instantly raged, I willingly grasped that as a positive.

CM Books, LLC

Chapter Nine

Keg

As I listened to Raven, I kept going back to the morning conversation with my sister. Things she said brought a new perspective to what Raven had chosen to do. I wasn't positive that if I'd been in her shoes, I wouldn't have made the same decision. So much was going on in her life at that time, could I hold it all against her? She was seventeen and pregnant with my child, and I'd dumped her easily because all I heard was that she was moving. Even though neither of us knew at the time. I couldn't even bring myself to hate the man that had given my son his last name. He stepped in and loved Ry as his own in my absence.

With my anger set aside, and the hurt, I processed all she had said. I'd ask the few questions I had, and then it was time to shove it all in the past. I couldn't focus on the time I missed with Ry when there was so much left ahead for us.

"If your husband hadn't died, do you think you would have ever told me or at least Ry and left it up to him?"

A tear from Raven's already glistening eyes rolled down her cheek, and she wiped it away before answering, "I don't know. When I talked with Ry, he asked a similar question. I'd like to think I would have. Keeping him from you did wear on me, Reed. Sometimes so much that Derek would tell me that it would be okay if I wanted to inform you, he'd be with me every step. I often wondered why he was so accepting of my decision, I never asked. But after his death when I'd think of our time together, I wondered if it had had anything to do with him being raised in foster care and never really having a family of his own. In his need to have a family, he would put up with anything or do anything to keep it. I'll never know, and that's probably best."

"How is Ry doing?"

"I was worried at first because he seemed to shut down. But after talking with him and answering his questions, he surprisingly took the information in stride." Her lips curved in a half smile.

"What's the smile for?"

"Something he said at dinner yesterday. Basically, it was that he now had the answer to his love for motorcycles, it was in his blood."

I couldn't help but laugh, and it felt great. "Glad to see the kid can keep his focus on things while shit's happening around him. Still working you for a dirt bike?"

"Yeah, any chance he can work it in a conversation. Ry's always had a fascination with motorcycles from the first time he saw one. He even has several models of motorcycles

CM Books, LLC

he's put together. No one can touch them but him. He has a panic attack if Reagan even goes near them."

Hearing about Ry's hobby reminded me about the boxes in my dad's shed. I wasn't looking forward to going through all my stuff stored there before now.

"We men are protective of our toys." I grinned, and she rolled her eyes. The few things she shared of Ry only touched the surface of my need to know about him. "Tell me more about Ry. I want to know everything."

"Surprisingly, I had an easy pregnancy. Ry was born at one thirteen in the morning and weighed eight pounds even. Twenty-one inches long and a full head of dark brown hair, he made his appearance into the world known, and he's never stopped. He's always been laid back, and I shouldn't have been surprised how easily he's dealing with this. Thinking about it, even when he was little, he dealt with things pretty much the same way. Going silent as if working it out in his head."

As Raven continued to share moments of Ry's life, I found myself absorbing each milestone and eager to learn more. The anger faded. The hurt would take a little longer, but I'd cope with it. I figured it too would eventually go away.

Not sure how long we talked, but the sun started going down in the sky and with it the warmth it provided. "I want to hear any and everything to do with Ry. However, I should probably get you back before the kids and your grandparents wonder what happened to you."

"I left a note. However, we should head back, it's cooling off, and I might not have been on a bike in years, but I do remember the difference in temps when the wind hits you."

I stood and gathered our trash and deposited it in the nearby trash. We were both quiet as we walked to where my bike was parked.

"I'm going to get hit with a hundred questions about getting to ride on your bike." Raven laughed, and when I looked at her, I didn't see the twenty-nine-year-old woman; I saw the young girl who had been everything to me. Sami's voice whispered inside my head. *You loved her once.*

I had loved her. And I wasn't sure I still didn't.

I stepped closer to Raven. "You can blame Sami."

My hands cupped her face, and I closed what little distance was between us. Tilting her face up and bending to meet her lips with mine, I kissed her. On her gasp I plunged my tongue in, her taste slamming into me. Gripping me. She'd been the only woman I'd ever taken my time with. If she affected me like that in our teens, what the hell would she do to me now?

The small moan that escaped her vibrated to my groin and more was what I thought. I wanted more of her.

She raised her hands to my chest and grasped my t-shirt. This was what I was missing out of life—her.

The sound of a car door closing grabbed my attention, reminding me we stood in the open in the parking lot of a park. Softening the kiss, I released her lips and placed soft kisses down her neck until my face pressed into the crook of her neck.

Raven leaned her head against me, and we both worked to gain some control. When I felt her body begin to shake, followed by the sound of her giggling, I straightened and looked down at her.

She tilted her head back to look at me. "You're going to have to tell me why Sami is to blame for that."

I grinned, kissed the top of her head then handed her a helmet. "Later. We need to get back."

Raven gave me a strange look but didn't press. I was glad she didn't because I wasn't sure what to tell her.

On the ride back to her grandparents, I went back and forth with the possibility that I could still love her even after everything.

We arrived back at Raven's grandparents' place. Raven said Ry was in acceptance of the drastic change in his life, but I needed to see for myself. If she was right, the kid definitely was working through it better than me.

"You okay, Reed?" At Raven's question, I realized she'd gotten off the bike while I still sat holding my helmet in my hands.

"Yeah, just wondering if I should give Ry more time to adjust. I didn't make the best impression yesterday. I don't want to mess this up before we even have a chance."

"You won't. Come on, only one way to see."

After getting off the bike, I followed Raven inside the house. The sound of voices could be heard from the kitchen, so Raven led us in that direction. When we walked through the doorway, four heads turned in our direction.

"Mommy, you're home!" Reagan smiled at her mom, then her eyes landed on me. "Are you going to yell at us some more?"

"Reagan!" Raven and her grandmother yelled at the same time.

"I hadn't planned to," I answered the little girl whose eyes and features were shared with her mom.

"Good, 'cause you're scary when you're mad."

Holding out my hand, I moved to the end of the table and shook hands with Doc Newhouse, who'd stood when we entered the kitchen.

"Nice seeing you, Doc."

"Been a long time, son."

"Reed, sit down and eat, there's plenty. Raven, get plates out for you and Reed."

"Thank you, ma'am." I waited until Raven returned to sit. She placed a plate in front of the empty spot next to Ry, then walked around the table and sat next to her daughter. I smiled at Ry as I sat. He hadn't taken his eyes off me since I entered, nor had he spoken.

"Sure smells good. I bet it even tastes better." I looked at Ry when I spoke. He nodded, then turned back to his food.

"Never had to worry about leftovers when you ate with us," Mrs. Newhouse said and smiled at me.

I chuckled as I filled my plate with meatloaf, mashed potatoes and gravy, and green beans.

CM Books, LLC

"My dad tried to cook for Sami and me after Mom passed. The food had been edible, but just barely. I always looked forward to eating your cooking, Mrs. Newhouse."

"Call me, Gretchen."

At the first taste of the meatloaf, it took everything in me not to moan. My cooking skills weren't much better than my dad's, and though the ol' ladies sometimes cooked at the clubhouse for us all, good meals were far and few between. Eating out didn't take long to get sick of either.

Raven told the kids to eat before the food got cold, so for a few minutes, everyone focused on eating instead of carrying on a conversation.

As I ate, Ry kept glancing toward me, and Reagan looked as though she was going to bounce out of her chair trying not to talk. I inwardly grinned because Ally was the same way.

It didn't take long for everyone to finish eating, and Raven started clearing the table.

"What's all that stuff on your vest mean?" Reagan pointed to my club vest after she came around the table and stood beside me.

I noticed Ry's interest in his sister's question and pushed my chair back enough to allow me room to move. I looked at Reagan, then at Ry, and pointed over my shoulder to the back of my vest.

"The skull in the middle is my club's symbol. The rocker underneath that says Washington, shows where the club is located. The downward rocker above the skull tells my position in the club, enforcer."

113

"What's that mean?" Ry asked.

"Well…" While I thought briefly on how to best explain, Doc coughed, and I cut my eyes to him. At his age, and how long Haven MC had been in the town, he'd know enough about the club. The smirk on his face told me I was right, and he was waiting to see how I explained my job. "As enforcer, I handle any problems that could harm the club, which includes even if a problem is caused by one of our members. The club has rules to follow, and members are required to follow them."

I grinned at Doc, feeling a little proud of myself until Reagan said, "Like a teacher. If I don't behave and follow the rules in my class, I get in trouble."

Doc snorted, and I'd bet anything it was because he was trying to picture me as a teacher. Hell, I was, too. Not sure what I could teach them that would make their parents happy.

"Geez, Reagan. They don't get recess taken away or not get a star for the day on their papers. They get their…a—butts kicked. Right?"

I wasn't verifying crap. I knew when I was out of my league, and luckily, Raven was done helping her grandmother clean up the kitchen and stepped in. "Ryker, you were told not to watch those shows. They aren't age appropriate for you. And not everything on television is true."

"Duh. I know that, Mom."

"I thought your name was Reed? That says Keg." Reagan pointed on my vest at the patch with Keg on it.

"My name is Reed, but my road name is Keg—it's what my club brothers call me."

"Why?" Ry asked.

"Well, when you first join the club, you're a prospect. And before you become a member, someone in the club will usually tag you with a name. Either from something you've done or how you act." I shrugged my shoulder.

Ry and Reagan seemed to accept that until Raven chuckled. She knew how I got the name because I was tagged with it not long after I started prospecting. I turned in the chair and narrowed my eyes at her. She smiled in return.

"Why don't you tell them how you earned yours," she said, biting her lip to keep from laughing and throwing me under the bus at the same time.

"Tell us," Reagan said and shocked me when she moved and climbed in my lap.

"Reagan, maybe Reed don't want you sitting in his lap," Ry said, and I didn't miss that he used my name for the first time.

"It's fine, Ry." Raven rubbed Ry's shoulder and stood behind his chair.

Ry tilted his head back, looking up at her. "Well, he's not her dad."

"Ryker Reed Allen, that is enough," Raven said and glared down at Ry.

I stiffened and sat frozen in the chair, caught off guard by hearing his full name for the first time.

I never asked, and Raven hadn't mentioned Ry's middle name when we talked in the park. She said several

115

times that she thought of me often and what she was doing to both Ry and me.

"Reagan, let's go get your jacket and walk down to the mailbox. I forgot to check the mail when we came home." Gretchen walked over and took Reagan's hand and helped her off my lap.

"Alright."

"I'll go, too. I could use the exercise after that meal," Doc said and stood. As he headed for the kitchen doorway, a dog came out from under the table and followed them out, giving the three of us privacy.

I looked at Raven, and she gave me a half smile and then stroked her hand over Ry's hair. He stared at me as if waiting to see how I would react.

"I had no idea…you never said his full name. I didn't ask." I ran my hand down my face, then around and rubbed the back of my neck.

"Are you mad I have your name?"

I turned in the chair until I faced him, then placed my hand on one leg above his knee. "Not in the least. I'm sorry my silence made you think otherwise. It just kinda hit me. You know?" I squeezed his leg.

"Yeah. It kinda hit me, too. Well…not when Mom yelled at me… Before…when."

I chuckled. "I get it, Ry."

"So, will you let me sit on your bike?" Ry asked, and Raven burst out laughing.

"Ah…no."

"Come on, I promise not to scratch it."

116

"I remember a kid who looked just like you telling your mom something about knowing how guys don't like their rides touched." I lifted my brows in question.

"Yeah, you're my dad, so you should let me."

The kid was a riot and his moods changed faster than I could keep up. Impassive, curious, indifferent, funny, even a little jealously surfaced over his sister getting on my lap.

"Nice try, kid." I chuckled. "You need to work on your game if you're going to hang with a bunch of bikers."

I received a full-fledged smile that if you took away the braces, it reminded me of my dad's. Wild Bill was going to love this kid.

"I get to hang out at the clubhouse?"

"Some. We have cookouts and celebrations that the families attend. We handle business there, and a few of the single guys live there, so there will be times you're not allowed to be there."

"Like when you have parties and the women who don't wear much clothes are there?"

Yeah, fatherhood was definitely going to be an experience. I was beginning to appreciate my dad a whole lot more. This kid would keep me on my toes.

"Oh my God, Ryker. I'm taking the television out of your room!"

I laughed at Raven's expense, and she lightly smacked my shoulder.

"Why'd you hit me? I didn't say it."

"You're encouraging him."

I gave her a 'what the hell' look. "I don't know how you came to that conclusion; I didn't say anything."

"You laughed!"

Ry and I both laughed and laughed harder when Raven glared at us.

"Oh, come on. Look at what you've missed the last twelve years." Raven's eye filled with moisture, and it hit me what I'd said. I stood and then bent until we were eye level. "It was a joke. A bad joke. I was trying to get you to laugh with us. I hadn't meant it as a dig."

"I know. It's just…standing here watching the two of you together. Laughing and picking on each other. I-I hadn't realized how much alike you both are." She looked between Ry and me. "I'm so very sorry that I cost both of you time together." Raven grabbed Ry's arm and pulled him up, then wrapped her arms around him. Hugging him. I stepped closer and encumbered the two of them with my arms.

"Starting now, it is done. No more should've, could've, would've. We focus on tomorrow and the next day. Understand?" I released them from my arms and stepped back.

Raven kissed Ry's forehead before letting him go. "Yes. If you can do that, so can I."

"Good. How about you, Ry?"

"Okay, but am I going to lose the television in my room or not?" I chuckled and reached my hand out, placing it on top of his head, then messing his hair up.

"On that note. I'm going to take off. Your grandparents and Reagan are probably waiting to come in."

"Nah, Gramps is probably letting Sabith run around," Ry said as Raven and he followed me out of the kitchen and to the front door.

Once we were outside, Ry and Raven walked with me to my bike in the driveway. As we reached it, Doc, Gretchen, and Reagan came around the corner of the garage with the dog traipsing behind them.

"What were you doing on the side of the garage?" Raven asked, and Doc pointed at the dog.

"Waiting on Sabith to come out of the woods. She must have heard or caught sight of a deer and decided to give a little chase," he answered Raven, then turned toward me. "You heading home?"

"Yeah. It's getting late. Thanks for feeding me, Mrs…Gretchen."

"You're always welcome here, Reed."

"Hey, you never told us how you got the name Keg," Reagan said, and Raven chuckled.

"No, I didn't. How about I share that later?"

"Okay. I'll remind you," she said and turned toward the house with her grandparents.

"If you're banking on her forgetting, you'd be wrong."

"I'll tell her tomorrow," I answered Raven, then looked down at Ry, who had ignored everyone because he was scoping out my bike. "Ry, tomorrow I thought I could pick you up and we could go to my dad's place. It's Sunday, and I usually hang out with him for a few hours. Afterward, we could swing by my house and have some dinner, then I'll bring you back."

"He's my grandad, right?"

"Yep."

"He was the one yesterday that rode up while we were stopped at the gate after…"

"That's him. Yesterday morning wasn't the best way for us to meet, but Ry, he and I are both looking forward to getting to know you."

"Okay then. He's big like you. Do you think I'll get as big?"

"I'd say you've gotten a good start on it already." I ruffled his hair. He was closing in on thirteen and was almost as tall as Raven.

"I'm taller than most of the boys in the middle school."

"It was like that for me at your age."

"You're dad, too?"

"I'm sure he was."

"You and he don't look much alike."

"Only our size and a few facial features. I got my hair color and eyes from my mom. But wait until you meet your aunt, my sister, Sami. She has our dad's hair and eyes, but our mom's height. You're probably as tall if not already taller than her."

"Does she live around here?"

"No, but she's only a few hours away."

"Does she know about me?"

"Oh yeah. It won't surprise me if she isn't already planning a visit."

"She got kids?"

"Ry, why don't you save some questions for tomorrow?" Raven chuckled.

"Alright." He sounded almost disappointed in not getting to find out more right then. I would answer any question the kid had, it was nice thinking he wanted to know just as much about me, and the people around me, as I did about him.

"That works. Well, I guess I'll head home and see you tomorrow." I placed my helmet on and mounted the bike. I glanced at Raven, where her and Ry stood after stepping away from the bike. "You and Reagan are welcome to come along, too," I said, thinking Ry might be more comfortable with them tagging along.

She smiled, and I knew she understood. "If Ry doesn't mind us butting in on his time, then yes." She looked and Ry. "Is it okay with you?"

I could see Ry's body physically relax. I didn't know how long it was going to take for him to be comfortable being alone with me. But as long as I was able to spend time with him, I didn't care.

"It's cool."

"Then we have a plan. I'll see you guys tomorrow." I fired the bike up, and after I maneuvered away from Raven's car, I threw up my hand up and headed down the driveway.

Once I reached my house, I pulled through the garage door and pulled out my cell to give my dad a heads up on tomorrow. After filling him in on the stuff I'd learned about Ry, I locked up and headed to bed. I closed my eyes, already looking forward to spending more time with Ry. And if I was honest with myself, Raven and Reagan, too.

CM Books, LLC

Chapter Ten

Raven

A four door truck I didn't recognize sat off to the side of the garage. I figured it had to belong to Reed. It was after eleven, and I wasn't sure when he was coming to pick us up. I parked in the drive and made my way inside. Hearing the kids laughing lightened my mood.

It was always hard losing an animal. The female dog from the shelter Gramps had worked on, and even stayed with the first night, died. Gramps said she made it through the first night and looked to be on the mend, though she had a way to go. Every day she survived her chances increased. I went in this morning with Gramps to help since we had three staying over for various medical reasons and several dogs and cats that were boarding with us. When we got in, Matt, the weekend helper, met us at the door. He'd gone in the room where the medical-kept patients were to clean up any messes in their kennels, and the female dog was struggling to breathe.

We immediately put oxygen on her while giving her a mild sedative so she wouldn't fight it. After examining her, we concluded she had a bleeder and her lungs were filling up with fluid. I prepped her for surgery, and Gramps got everything needed together. Gramps found the bleeder and was preparing to fix it when she died on the table. The poor baby had given up the fight.

"Hey, Mom," Ry said as I walked into the living room. Keg sat on the couch with Gran, and Ry and Reagan were on the floor.

"Hey. Sorry, I'm running a little late. I hope you haven't been waiting long."

"Nah, you're good. Only been here about fifteen minutes," Reed said and looked back at the others. "Ry and Reagan were telling me about their teachers and school while we waited on you."

"Good. Let me wash up and change my shirt, and I'll be ready to leave."

"Where's Gramps?" Reagan asked and leaned as if to see around me.

"He had a few things to finish, then he'll be home."

"Then, I best get lunch ready. He'll be hungry when comes in. Do any of you want anything?" Gran asked and stood.

I looked toward Keg. "Do you want to eat lunch here? I know we are going by your dad's, but I wasn't sure what time you were coming."

"I probably should have told you that my dad cooks lunch on Sunday. It's our thing. We got in the habit of it since it's just him and me."

I smiled. "I remember eating at your house a few times. Has he gotten better?"

"Nowhere near Getchen's cooking, but he doesn't do too bad. He's learned if you keep it simple, it comes out edible."

"Wise man. If you'll be home for dinner, honey, let me know, okay?"

"I know I mentioned to Ry about eating at my house, but I thought I'd take you guys out to dinner instead."

"Oh, okay," I answered Reed, then looked at Gran. "Then, no, we won't be home for dinner."

"Then you all have fun. See you when you get back," Gran said and headed out of the room.

"Where are we going to eat dinner at?" Ry asked as he got up off the floor.

"Ry, you haven't even eaten lunch yet," I said and laughed.

"Just planning ahead, Mom."

"I thought you might like to go to Lugio's Pizza and Arcade."

Reagan jumped up and down, and Ry punched his fist in the air.

Reed looked at the kids, then to me. "Going for the long shot and guess they've been there."

"Yes, a few times. They love pizza, but the arcade inside—"

Ry and Reagan cut me off and finished my sentence. "Makes it double the fun," they said together.

"Yes, it does," Reed said, I lifted a brow when he looked at me.

"No way you go to that place. It's loud and filled with kids yelling and running around," I said.

"Best pizza in town. Me and a few brothers go at least every other month to eat and play the games in the arcade. If we don't want to put up with the craziness, we call it in and pick it up. What can I say? Sometimes we're just big kids." He shrugged, and I chuckled.

I chuckled, then turned toward the stairs. "Give me a couple of minutes and I'll be ready."

As we walked into Reed's dad's home, memories hit me of the few times Reed and I had come back to his house, skipping school after Sami and his dad had left. We'd spend the time we should have been in school in his bedroom, then we'd leave before Sami was due home, and he'd drop me off at Gramps and Gran's place like he did every day after school. There was a good chance Ry was conceived in Reed's bedroom.

"Mom!" Ry yelled, and I turned to see they were in the hall standing in front of pictures while I still stood at the entrance gazing up the stairs, reliving what seemed a lifetime ago.

The smirk on Reed's face told me he knew what I was thinking. "Had a few good times here, didn't we, Rav?" He's words verified I was right.

CM Books, LLC

With the kids listening and watching, I smiled. "Yes, we did. I loved coming here."

"Here are pictures of Reed and his sister, Mom." I walked to Ry so I could see what he was looking at. Reed stood by his bike with a big grin on his face, and a young Sami stood beside him with her arm stretched behind his head, making bunny ears with her fingers.

"She's pretty," Reagan said, and I turned to see who she was talking about and saw it was another picture of Sami, standing by a car with keys dangling from her fingers.

"Sami had just gotten her license in that pic," Reed said.

Reagan looked at Ry and her eyebrow furrowed, and her nose crinkled. "You kinda look like her, Ry."

"I don't look like a girl."

"Yeah, you do, but you really look like him," Reagan said and pointed to a picture that I remembered seeing before. It was of Reed and his dad and mom. His dad was dressed in a military uniform and held Reed who was still a toddler.

Staring at the picture, I could see what Reagan did. "You do, Ry. How old was your dad in that picture?"

"I'm not sure. Twenty-one, twenty-two," Reed answered as a door slammed.

"Hey! You're here. Why didn't you come out back?" Mr. Borelli stood in the doorway of the kitchen. I'd been upset when he'd talked to me the other day at Haven and I hadn't taken a good look at him. If Reed was close on his dad's age in the picture, he had to be in his mid to late fifties.

127

Other than some gray working through at his temples, he looked the same. I thought when I dated Reed, he was good looking, now was no different. The man was aging like a fine wine.

"You could pass as Reed's brother," I blurted, then I felt my face grow hot from blushing.

Reed snorted, and his dad threw back his head and laughed. "Darlin', if you're going to pass out those type of compliments, please keep coming over. You make an old man feel good."

"Ry looks like you." Reagan, who never met a stranger and had no filter, decided to join the conversation.

"Hey, Dad. That's Reagan, and this is Ryker."

His dad looked down at Reagan and smiled. "Nice to meet you, sweetheart. And you look like your momma."

Reagan, who usually wasn't shy, shocked me by stepping back and put an arm around my waist and leaning into my side.

"Nice to meet you, Ryker. Hear you prefer Ry?" Mr. Borelli stuck out his big hand, and Ry hesitantly placed his in to shake hands.

"Either, but most people call me, Ry." I gave him a little nudge. "Sir."

Reed chuckled, and I glared at him.

"Ry, it is."

"What do I call you…sir?"

"I guess whatever you're comfortable with. My granddaughter calls me papa. You can call me that or any of the other of the names set aside for grandfathers. You can even call Prez or Wild Bill. I'll answer to any of them."

"Prez means you're the president of the club." Ry's eyes went to the vest Mr. Borelli had on that was like Reed's. "You are the president; it says it on your vest. Reed told us what everything stood for. Wow, it's just like on the television shows." Ry glanced at me with 'see' look, then turned to Reed. "You're his son, and I'm yours. On the show, the son takes over when the dad steps down, or he gets killed."

"Ry, I am so taking the TV out of your room." I looked at Reed's dad. "I'm so sorry, Mr. Borelli."

"Don't worry about it, Raven. I've caught a few episodes myself. Wanted to see what all the hype was about." Reed's dad was smiling, and I was glad he didn't get upset over Ry's comment.

"Really, you watched them, Wild Bill?"

Well, it seemed Ry had chosen what he was going to call his grandfather.

"A couple times. You know not to believe everything you see on TV, right?"

"Yes, sir."

"Good, now come on. I cooked burgers on the grill, and the French fries should just about be finished in the oven."

"Okay. Come on, Reagan," Ry said and grabbed her hand. She let go and went with Ry, both following Reed's dad like he was the pied piper. Ry had always been good about including her, even when he didn't really want her tagging along.

"I think Dad has an admirer."

"You probably don't see it because he is your dad, but when he enters a room, he brings a powerful presence with him. So do you."

Reed didn't reply, he just put his hand at the small of my back, leading me toward the kitchen. I had only taken a couple steps when I abruptly stopped in front of a picture.

"Oh my God, I can't believe this is hanging on the wall." It was Reed and I dressed up for his senior prom. I was only a sophomore and I'd talked him in to going, telling him everyone had to go to their senior prom. "You hadn't wanted to go."

"No, I had no desire to go."

"But you went and even dressed up. Black tie and all." I touched the picture. Reed had on a black jacket, white shirt, and black tie. I was dressed in a silver strapless gown that was fitted down to my waist, then flared out. "God, I felt so grown up."

"You looked beautiful that night. And I went because you wanted to go."

"I wanted you to have that memory. And it ended up being mine. I didn't go to my junior prom because I left to help Mom and finished the year homeschooled. Th…"

"And then you did homeschool for your senior year because you were pregnant with Ry," Reed said, finishing what I was started.

"Yeah." I looked over my shoulder at Reed. "I wouldn't go back and change it, even if I could. Well, maybe the part of keeping him from you. But you know what?"

"What?"

"If I'd done it differently, I wouldn't have Reagan. I can't imagine my life without her."

The look on Reed's face was one I caught several times when he looked at me, I wished I knew what he was thinking or that he'd tell me, but each time, he stayed silent. "Let's go see if Dad and the kids left us any food."

As we reached the kitchen, I caught the last of what Wild Bill said, "—across the field in front of all the families who attended to see their sons and daughters graduate." Then Ry's laughter and Reagan's little girl giggles followed.

"I know you did not tell them that story," Reed said, looking at his dad, shaking his head. Wild Bill replied with laughter.

"Uh huh, he said he was dared, so he stripped down to his skivvy and ran across a field where people were graduating, then they called him Wild Bill for doing it," Reagan said through giggles, which made me smile because I was sure she had no idea what skivvy meant.

"Reagan, you don't even know what skivvy means. It's underwear." Ry chuckled.

I should have figured Ry would know the meaning and share it with his sister. He was enthralled with military movies, cowboy movies, and the television series with bikers even knowing I didn't want him to watch them.

Reed and I joined them at the table, and when everyone had what they needed, we ate in silence for approximately one minute.

"Now, can you tell us how you got your name, Reed?" Ry asked.

"Yes! You said you'd tell us later," Reagan reminded him.

I raised my brows at Reed, and he smiled. "Yes, I did. So eat, and when you're finished, I'll tell you."

"Okay!" Reagan picked up her burger and took a big bite.

"Slow down before you choke," I scolded, looking between Reagan and Ry, so they knew it included them both.

"Raven, how're Doc and Gretchen doing?"

I told Wild Bill about Gramps' plan to retire and that both were doing well. Reed asked if I would miss being a predominantly large animal vet. We talked about the area and how it had changed in the time I'd been gone. Wild Bill even asked about Raleigh and if I'd enjoyed living there.

Visiting with Wild Bill had worried me when Reed asked if Reagan and I would like to spend the day with him and Ry. I knew he offered for Ry's sake, but I didn't want to bring tension into the first outing Reed and Ry shared. The worry I'd felt had been unwarranted. It felt like having a typical lunch with family, enjoyable and relaxing.

I was glad I'd agreed to come

CM Books, LLC

Chapter Eleven

Keg

"I'm done. Can you tell us the story now?" Ry asked.

"Me, too," Reagan said around the last bite of hamburger she'd shoved in her mouth.

I grinned across the table at Ry and Reagan. It felt like I'd known the two forever, and it had only been a little over forty-eight hours. I wiped my mouth and took a drink of my tea.

"Quit stalling. If you aren't going to tell, I will." My dad was enjoying himself. It was usually only him and me on Sundays with the occasional drop-in by one of the brothers. We'd eat, talk, then hang out and watch TV. If the weather was nice, we'd take a ride together. So, having Raven and the kids at the house was not only doing him good, it was uplifting for me, too.

"I'll tell them."

Raven chuckled. "I don't know why you're hesitant. It's funny."

"It's embarrassing."

"Only 'cause it happened to you. If it would have been one of the others, you would be telling everyone who missed seeing it." My dad was right, I would have.

"Alright. I told you how the prospects get tagged with names." At their nods, I continued, "Well, as a prospect, you are always doing some type of work or running errands or any other thing no one else in the club wants to do. I'd been prospecting for a couple months, and I finally was getting a night off. The club was having a party that night and supplies needed to be picked up. Pinch, who was a prospect then too, and I were sent to pick everything up: meat for the grill, chips, nuts, alcohol. Anything they needed.

"After Pinch and I do this, we take it back to the clubhouse and we had to unload it. I wanted to get the job done fast because it was the last thing I had to do before I could leave. I was going to see your mom.

"To save time, I decided to carry two containers of beer at one time. One on each shoulder. The containers are round and a little tall. They look like cylinders." I showed the size using my hands. "One of the cylinders weighs around eighty-seven pounds. I pulled one from the truck and hoisted it on my shoulder. It wasn't heavy as much as an awkward fit because of the bulkiness.

"After I had one situated, Pinch lifted another one and placed it on my other shoulder. I held them by the handle on top. The two together were only a hundred and seventy-four pounds. For my size, even though I wasn't as

CM Books, LLC

big as I am now, the combined weight was nothing for me to carry.

"I carried the two to where they were supposed to go, so they could be set up for the party, then returned for the last two. Pinch helped again and positioned the second one for me. This time, though, when I stepped away from the truck, the one on the left shifted and started to roll off my shoulder. I leaned to the right side trying to get it to roll back in place.

"It didn't work. The other one began to roll, and before I could stop it, they both rolled off my shoulders and landed on the ground. When they first hit the ground, nothing happened. In the next minute, the pressure had built inside from the shaking of all that beer."

"Like shaking a can of soda?" Ry asked.

"Exactly. The seal broke on the cap top, it's where you put the nozzle in that dispenses the beer. The cap blew, spraying gallons of beer in every direction as the containers spun." I used the salt shaker on the table to give the kids a visual.

Ry was listening with a smile on his face, but Reagan was frowning as if she didn't understand. Which for her age and the topic, she shouldn't understand. Ry maybe knew a little, picking some up from the TV. At least I hoped he had no experience, then I cringed a little inside as I thought about him being an official teen in a few months.

"The containers of beer are called kegs. So after that, everyone started calling me Keg, and it stuck."

Reagan pursed her lips. "Wild Bill's story was funnier."

Ry looked at me and said, "It was kinda…boring."

I shrugged. "You wanted to know. And that's it."

"Yeah, I just thought…"

"It'd be more interesting?"

"Well, on—"

I raised my hand and cut Ry off. "Kid, you really need to quit watching those shows."

Dad laughed. "The part your da…Reed left out was him getting soaked along with some of the guys who had already arrived in preparation for the party. They were all jumping around dodging the canisters and the spraying beer."

"Did they get mad at you?"

It helped that my son's voice was filled with concern. I usually avoided the story when asked by the prospects. It'd been plain embarrassing for me. As the president's son, I thought I had to be better than any of the other prospects. That it was expected of me. But the ribbings I'd received over the accident was in good fun and showed me that they didn't look at me any different than any other prospect.

"They weren't too happy and told me in a few choice words. But accidents happen, and they eventually laughed about."

"Did you get to see him covered in beer?" Ry asked his mom, and I turned my head to look at her. Her nose was crinkled, but her eyes held humor.

"He'd put on dry clothes before he showed up, but he still reeked like he'd taken a bath in beer."

"Hey, in my defense, I was more interested in spending time with you."

"Aww, that's sweet. Still, it didn't help when you took me to the movies and we received all those looks." Raven stood and started clearing the table.

"You don't have to do that, sweetheart. I'll get to it later."

"It won't take but a few minutes. Consider it as my thank you for allowing me and the kids to join you today. Besides, you cooked."

Watching her interact with my dad, the three of them sharing a table with us—felt normal when it was anything but. Wanting her was easy, and I did want her.

Wouldn't a shrink have a field day inside my head? Hate and love were said to be closely related, I finally understood it.

I stood, needing my feet on solid ground. "While we're here and I have some cheap labor with me today." I looked at Ry and winked, then turned back to my dad. "I thought I'd haul a few of my boxes out of the storage shed."

"Sounds good. If I could get Sami to come and get her crap, I might get to store some of my things in there, instead of the garage."

"Good luck with that. With Ally in school and her pregnant, not sure when they'll find the time to make a trip here. Though she's dying to meet Ry, so she might pop in anytime. But if you really want the shed cleared out, we could load her stuff and take it to her."

"I don't have any plans for the shed. Just like giving you and her a hard time about it."

"All done," Raven said as she crossed the kitchen and stopped behind Reagan's chair. "Need any more help with toting boxes? I can pitch in."

"Me, too," Reagan added.

"Well, then I guess we should get started since I have such eager helpers. I'll even pay you with pizza and tokens later."

"You were already taking us there. How is that pay?" Ry questioned. The kid was sharp, I'd give him that.

Dad stood. "As fun as it sounds. I think I'll ride over to the club and leave you all to it."

I frowned. "You need me?"

"You're good. A couple things to take care of, and I want to check on Freak."

I could tell Dad wasn't wanting to talk in front of Raven and the kids about club business. Raven picked up on it, too.

"Come on, kids. Let's go outside while we wait for Reed."

"I'll be right behind you. I need to grab the key to the shed first."

"Take your time." She and the kids started toward the back door.

"In case you are gone before I get back, it was good seeing, Raven. Enjoyed having you and the kids here." My dad laid one hand on Ry's shoulder and one on Reagan's. "Looking forward to getting to know you both better." He removed his hands from their shoulders and reached in his pocket and pulled out money. Wild Bill always had cash in a clip. "Here you go. Play some arcade games on me," he said and handed a twenty to Ry and a twenty to Reagan. "Anytime you want to come over, you let Reed or your mom know, okay?"

Ry and Reagan nodded and thanked him for the money. Raven hugged him, and I watched them as they walked out the back door, then asked, "What's going on? If you need me at the club, I can run Raven and the kids home and meet you there."

"I'm meeting with Tram, Crank, and Pinch. After you left the funeral yesterday," we both smirked at his use of funeral for Freak's snake, "I sent Crank and Pinch on a little recon to see if they spotted any Widows out and about. Tram was going home to do his thing on the computer and see what he could find out on their leader, T-bone, so he'll be there to update. And I do want to check on Freak. Also, we're going to do inventory for the clubhouse. That way Latch and Mac can pick up supplies next week. Friday night's party is for Taylor being patched in. Which reminds me that soon at one of the meetings, I'm going to want all your opinions on if you think Latch is ready to patch in. Oh, and I got the names of two guys looking for a home from General Patel. They'll both be retiring soon, and they ride. I'll get more info on them from the General and have it at the next meeting, too. Today's stuff is nothing pressing, so I'll catch you, Moose, and Hawk up later. No sense for you three changing personal plans when you don't need to."

"Club is family. I can see with Moose and Hawk because they have ol' ladies. I don't."

"Bullshit, son. You've eaten and slept the club since you pulled on that vest as a prospect. And I let you because I was doing the same thing. After your mom died, it was easier to work on Haven's issues back then than it was to deal with the pain of losing her. If she were still here, I wouldn't be going into the club to handle shit that can wait until tomorrow or at the next meeting. If we were making plans to hit the Widows or backing up the Chief, you all would be in attendance no matter what time of day or what day it is."

"Club is twenty-four/seven. It's not a nine to five, Monday through Friday, Dad."

"You're right. But it doesn't have to consume your every thought. It's balancing, Reed. You're going to have to learn to balance between the club family and regular family now. There is club. There is family. And there is the ability to combine the two, so they can coexist. Pick one over the other, and you will fail both. Get me."

"Yeah, I get it."

"Good. The key to the shed is in the drawer, same as always. Lock up when you leave."

"I will. Ride safe."

"Always." Dad started to walk off and stopped and turned. "I watched you watching her with the same look you had for her before she moved. I also see the hesitation on your part."

"I want her, just not sure it's enough. And I sure don't want to start something with the potential to go bad and the repercussions from thinking with my dick, harm what I'm trying to build with Ry."

"I can understand that. But what if it works? Look at what you could have. Besides, I've never known you not to go after what you want." Dad didn't even wait for a reply, he turned and walked out. I grabbed the key out of the kitchen junk drawer and then did the same and walked out.

Outside, Raven, Ry, and Reagan were sitting in the chairs around the unlit fire pit in the middle of the yard.

"I always wanted one of these. I bet it is nice sitting out here when it's cold and roasting marshmallows and making s'mores."

"I'm not sure about those, but hot dogs come out real good." I walked past them heading toward the shed, then yelled over my shoulder, "Come, helpers, let's see what awaits us!"

"That is a lot of stuff to take to the dump."

I had to agree with Ry. "I'll get a couple of the prospects to haul the stuff away."

"These cards are neat. Some look old. You must have collected them a long time."

"For a few years. I've always liked baseball. When next season starts, would you like to go see a game? We could go watch the Mariners play."

"That'd be cool. I've never been to any professional sports games before."

141

"Then, we'll definitely go."

We opened box after box of my stuff, and though I had no plans to admit to my dad he was right, I agreed with him, too—it was mostly crap. He should have made Sami and me go through the junk years ago. We made two stacks, a dump stack, and a keep stack. The keep side consisted of two boxes with baseball cards, which Ry was flipping through, a few action figures, and various pictures taken of friends and family. The dump pile needed no explanation.

"Uh…have you ever thrown anything out?" Raven said and laughed.

"Hey, at one time or another, everything in here had importance and meant something to me," I said with the straightest face I could muster.

"Even this bag of rocks." The expression on Reagan's face as she looked down at the plastic bag filled with rocks she was holding in her hands, left me unable to keep a straight face.

"Well, I think I was younger than you when I collected those. Maybe six. I lived in Germany at the time. My dad was in the military then, and he was stationed overseas. I collected the rocks to bring back to the States with me."

"Ookaay." Reagan's drawn out response fitted her facial expression perfectly.

What I hoped to find amongst the boxes hadn't been located. There was only one box left on the side of the shed where my things were. I removed the tape and folded back

CM Books, LLC

the flaps and was disappointed it didn't have what I was looking for. It did contain a few items I'd forgotten about.

"Ooh, a teddy bear. It's so cute in its outfit," Reagan exclaimed.

The bear was dressed in a military uniform, and I smiled thinking of why I had gotten it.

"Wild Bill gave it to me before he deployed. His unit was going to be gone for six months. He told me all I had to do was talk to it while he was away, and he would hear me."

"Did he really hear you?" Reagan asked.

"I never asked him when he came home. But talking to Sergeant Bear made missing my dad a little easier."

"I miss my daddy sometimes," Reagan said, and I could have kicked myself for making her sad.

"Would you like Sergeant Bear? He's a great listener."

"Do you think if I talk to him, my daddy will hear me all the way in Heaven?"

"I'm not sure, Reagan. But would talking to Sergeant Bear make you feel better?"

She nodded.

"Then his is yours, sweetheart. Sergeant Bear needs a place to stay other than in a box. And I know you'll take good care of him." I held the bear out to her.

"Uh huh," she said, and gingerly took the bear from my hands and pulled him into her chest.

"What do you tell Reed, Reagan?" Raven made eye contact with me and smiled. The look in her eyes tightened my groin. I should've never kissed her. Since then, I've fought off the urges to kiss her again. My resolve diminished more each time I was around her.

"Thank you, Reed. I promise to take care of him."

"You're welcome. Well, two boxes aren't much to tote to the truck. We can handle that, don't you think, Ry?"

"Yep. Are we going now?"

"Might as well. I was looking for something I wanted to show you, but they weren't in any of the boxes. Another day when I'm here, I'll look in the garage."

"Some boxes could be mixed with Sami's stuff," Raven said and walked to the other side of the shed and moved down the row of Sami's things.

"Possibly, but who knows where in the stacks. She has twice as much stuff stored in here. I'll look another day for them, it's no big deal. We've been in here a few hours, and I want to swing by my house before we go to Lugio's. By then, everyone should be hungry."

"I could eat," Ry offhandedly said while he put the cards away and closed the lid on the box.

I chuckled. "I'm not surprised."

"Hey, I'm still growing."

"Wouldn't want to be responsible for stunting your growth." I ruffled his hair as I passed.

"Reed, I think I found one that might be yours. I see part of the R, but the rest is blocked by the boxes in front of it."

I turned to see Raven stretched on her tiptoes, trying to move the top box on a stack of five. Other than the possibility the whole pile would fall and land on her, the position had her t-shirt pulled up enough; it showed the small indention of the lower back above her jeans that were strained across her ass. It took everything in me not to groan out loud.

"You're going to pull the whole pile over on you." I grabbed her waist and held on until she was flat on her feet. "Let me do that."

Starting at the top and setting aside two boxes, I saw the box Raven was trying to get to. It was mine. I moved a couple other of Sami's things until I could lift the box and set it down. Beside it was another one of mine.

Once my two additional boxes were pulled, I placed Sami's back in place. These had to be what I was looking for. The weight of the boxes made it almost a guarantee.

"Hey, Ry. Why don't you open these?"

Raven looked at me questionably, and I smiled. She'd definitely forgotten these had been in my bedroom on shelves my dad had made to display them on. Then again, we'd been in my room for a different purpose.

Ry, without question, ripped the tape off both box tops, then pulled the tops back, revealing what the boxes contained. Lined from bottom to top in each box were motorcycles of different styles and eras encased in their own clear display case. I'd collected them for years. There had to be at least forty.

"Look, Mom. Reed puts together models, too." Raven and Reagan bent to look in the boxes, and Ry looked up at me. "I have models, too."

"Your mom told me you liked putting them together. It's actually what made me remember these were out here."

I bent down and picked one up. "I wish I had the skills it took to put these together, but unfortunately, I don't. These were handcrafted by others; I found some or others were given to me by my parents whenever they came across one. My mom loved thrift shops, garage sales, and antique shops. If a place had deals, she was there. She was the one who gave me the first one because I was fascinated with my dad's motorcycle. This is the one that she gave me and started my collection." I handed Ry the one I had taken out of the box.

"Why are they out here? Do you still collect them?" he asked while he turned the case around in his hands, inspecting the motorcycle that was inside.

"No. Not since I was fourteen."

"How come?"

"Well…" as always, when I thought of my mom, a lump formed in my throat. I swallowed to try to clear it, then forged on as three sets of eyes where suddenly on me, waiting, "it was kinda a thing between my mom and me. I was fourteen, and after she died, I lost interesting in collecting them."

"Oh," Ry said and set the case back in the box.

I looked down at the little arms that tried to encircle my waist. "You can have Sergeant Bear back if you want," Reagan said as she looked up at me. Her offer to give back the bear, in her little way of trying to comfort me, would be

CM Books, LLC

the moment I remembered where Reagan captured a piece of my heart with a simple gesture.

"Nah, you keep Sergeant Bear, sweetheart."

"Okay. But you can visit him when you want."

"Good deal. Now, how about we get these boxes loaded in my truck and dropped off at my house, so we can go have some fun." I glanced at Raven and she smiled, making me wonder if she knew what had just happened with her daughter and me.

"I think that is a great idea," she said and ran a hand down from my shoulder to forearm, giving it a squeeze.

Yeah, she knew.

"I still can't get over your house. It's absolutely beautiful, Reed."

"Thanks, Raven. I know the place is big for just me, but I couldn't pass up the deal I got on it. I still need to buy some furniture. But I think I'll start with getting the downstairs fixed up before I worry about the four empty bedrooms upstairs. Well, the three that will still be empty after I set one up for Ry. Can't have him sleeping on the couch." I winked at Ry.

When we swung by my house to drop off the stuff from my dad's, I showed them around. While I was showing them the upstairs, I told Ry that once he felt comfortable with me, I'd like him to stay over at the house sometimes.

His immediate response of, *'Sure, where will I sleep, though?'* surprised me, and I think Raven, too. After the initial shock, I told him to pick. He went through each bedroom again before making his choice.

After finishing the tour, we loaded back up in my truck and headed for Lugio's. I'd felt stupid for every minute I had worried whether Ry would be genuinely interested in a father/son relationship with me or even if he wanted to put in the effort. His agreeing to stay at the house was like saying he was willing to try. It was all I could expect for right now.

"I wouldn't worry about those rooms either. It gives you time to think about what you want to put in them. You could make one a computer room or office. Even a room to exercise in if you want. After seeing your place reminded me I really need to get busy finding a house for us. I know Gran and Gramps don't mind us staying there, but it will be nice to have our own space. I'll be in the same boat as you with furniture. I didn't want to move a full house of furniture here and have it shoved in storage until I found a place. So I sold everything but a few pieces that I didn't want to part with, and they're in storage with everything we kept."

"Wow, you're going to be doing a lot of shopping."

"Yes, we're going to need a lot of stuff."

"She even got rid of mine and Reagan's beds," Ry added in between bites of pizza.

"You needed new beds anyway."

"Can we come over to your house again and swim in the pool?" Reagan asked as she reached for her drink.

"You sure can. But you're going to have to wait until summer to swim, though."

148

"The woods behind your house would be a great place to ride a dirt bike," Ry said, giving Raven a huge smile.

"Gee, Ry, no one would even know you want a dirt bike. You haven't mentioned it…" Raven pretended to look at her watch, and I laughed, "…in roughly twenty-four hours."

"Well, they would be. It would give me something to do when I stay over. And if you're worried about me learning to ride, Mom—who better to teach me than Reed. You know, since he rides a bike."

I felt my lips twitch and fought not to laugh at the kid. He was really working on his mom.

"Ryker, you should be ashamed of yourself using Reed in your relentless pursuit of a dirt bike."

"You've got to admit his angle was priceless." I couldn't help but laugh.

"Don't you start, too."

I held my hands up in surrender at Raven and winked at Ry.

"I saw that, mister."

"I don't know what you're talking about."

"Uh huh." Raven eyed me, and I smirked. She huffed, then looked at a grinning Ry and Reagan. "Eat if you want to have time to play in the arcade. You have school tomorrow."

That was all that needed to be said to get the two kids focused on finishing their food.

Raven sighed while I shook my head at Ry. He'd shoved the last piece of pizza in his mouth and talked around it. "Can we go in the arcade now?"

149

Other than the physical differences between a girl and a boy, I hadn't thought much about any others. Even having grown up with a sister. Until I looked over at Reagan to see if she was finished and noticed how she politely sat chewing her pizza. When she was done, she took a drink of soda, then picked up her napkin and wiped her mouth. I glanced back at Ry and watched him grab the neck of his t-shirt and wipe his mouth on it. Looking at the two them, it hit me the age difference between Ry and Reagan was about the same as mine and Sami's.

Watching them also reminded me of something my mom once said to my dad. I'd told Sami that all girls smelled. She yelled they did not, and we went back and forth until my dad had had enough and told us boys and girls both smelled. My mom had turned to him laughing and said, *"Little girls are sweet and smell clean, and little boys are mean and stinky."* Sami and I had been about the same age then as Ry and Reagan were now, too. I grinned at the thought that maybe my mom had been right.

Sliding out of the booth, I asked, "Who's ready to race cars and lose?"

"You, 'cause I rule at racing," Ry said as he stood.

"Come on, Reagan. You and I will find something for you to play while they race each other." Raven took Reagan's hand after she was out of the booth.

"Hey, don't be in such a hurry. We can take turns. Next person up takes on the winner of mine and Ry's challenge," I said, not wanting Reagan to feel left out. Then I looked at Ry and smirked, "Which, of course, will be me."

CM Books, LLC

"I can't play the race game. My legs don't reach the pedals," Reagan said as we walked through the arcade doors.

"How about you help me kick your brother's cocky little ass? You can steer from my lap and I'll work the foot pedals?"

"Yay! Let's kick Ry's cocky little ass," Reagan yelled, and a few adults passing by with their kids turned their heads and glared. When their eyes hit my vest, they faced forward and hurried away.

"Reagan!" Raven whispered yelled. A skill I think only mothers possessed.

"Sorry," Reagan said, then glanced at me. I winked at her, and she grinned, then walked away with Ry toward two empty chairs at the racing consoles.

"If you so much as laugh, Reed Borelli."

"Do I look like I'm laughing?" I asked and bit the inside of mouth to keep from doing just that.

"So help me if she repeats that at school and they call…I'm going to give them your number so you can talk to them and explain where she heard it."

"Then you might as well give me her teacher's name and the number to the school. Because after she spends any time around my brothers, it will be inevitable that the school will call." I did laugh then and received a swat to the shoulder for it.

"Come on, Mom and Reed, we're growing old over here," Ry yelled over his shoulder.

Raven groaned. "Please tell me it gets better."

I chuckled. "Yeah, I could if you want me to lie."

"Great."

I draped my arm over her shoulders. "We better get moving. I can see him graying from here."

"Jerk."

I hadn't laughed so much in one day. Maybe my dad was right—I could balance everything—Raven, kids, family, and club. Something I needed to think about.

"Those two are going to sleep good tonight."

"Hell, them. I will," I answered Raven, and she laughed.

There wasn't a game in the arcade we didn't play in the hour and a half we stayed. On the drive back to Doc's house, Reagan even fell asleep and Raven had to shake her awake once we got to the house.

"You sure you don't want to come in?" Raven asked.

"I'm sure." If we hadn't been standing on her grandparents' porch, and this was her place, I would have said yes. Which probably would have been a huge mistake for both of us.

"Well, I guess I'll see you next week when you visit Ry."

"Yeah. I hope Doc and Gretchen don't get sick of seeing me."

"You know they won't. What you should worry about is the weight you're going to put on with Gran feeding you. I won't be surprised if she bakes this week knowing you are going to be here."

CM Books, LLC

I groaned. "I won't even mind the extra workouts if she makes those triple fudge brownies. As many as I ate, I should've weighed five hundred pounds back then."

"Her cooking is another reason I need to find the kids and me a place. If I don't, I going to put more weight on top of the extra I already carry."

I looked her over. "You look great, Raven. A few extra pounds won't change that, it's just extra cushion."

"Thank you. But underneath my clothes is the body of a mother of two."

"Don't say shit like that about yourself. Ain't a damn thing wrong with your body."

"You're being nice, and I appreciate it. You took it the wrong way, though. I'm perfectly fine with my body. But after having Ry and Reagan, I'm carrying a few extra pounds that won't go away, and I'm good with it."

"Good, you should be. Now, I better get going."

"Okay, see you later."

I walked down the steps of the porch and toward my truck, then stopped and stood there for a minute.

"Did you forget something?" Raven called out, and I turned around, walked back toward the house and up the stairs to the porch, stopping in front of her.

"Yeah, I did."

Before I put any more thought into it, I put a hand on her neck and the other at her waist and yanked her against me. Her eyes widened, then closed as I took her mouth. I pushed my tongue past her lips and tasted every crevice of her mouth.

I moved my hand and gripped her butt, pressing her closer. Letting her feel the hardness behind my jeans and capturing her moan as I savaged her mouth.

Kissing Raven was like coming home.

I eased up, softening the kiss. Relaxing the hold I had on her until I finally lifted my lips from hers. I waited for her to open her eyes, and when she did, I saw everything I needed to know.

Stepping away from her, I turned and walked down the stairs.

"Was Sami to blame for that one, too?"

I grinned as I reached my truck and opened the door. "Nah, it was all me. Night, Raven," I said, then got in my truck, pulled the door closed, and after starting it up, I drove away.

Looked as if I was going after what I wanted.

Chapter Twelve

Raven

"Gets me worked up, then goes home. One minute he's kissing me, the next he's playing a game on the floor with Ry and Reagan. A week and he has me talking to an empty room. Ugh, the damn man."

"What'd you say, Raven?" Gramps asked from the doorway, startling me.

"Oh, nothing. I was counting out loud," I answered, not turning around to look at him because no way would I admit my sexual frustration to my grandfather.

"Is that the antibiotics for the Great Dane?"

"Yes, he has an ear infection. Gave him his yearly shots, and they're scheduling a teeth cleaning."

"Alright. Well, I guess I'll take off then. Will you be okay for the rest of the afternoon by yourself? I can stay if you need me to."

"There's no reason for you to stay, Gramps. It's been a slow Friday, and I don't imagine we'll have a mad rush of patients this afternoon. And if we do, I think I can handle it." I twisted the cap on the pill bottle and turned and faced him. "You are supposed to be cutting back your hours, you know."

"Yeah, yeah. Not sure what I'm going to do with my time once I retire."

"You could always take Gran on a trip. Take up fishing or just sit around with your feet up. Sleep in for a change." The look I got from Gramps made me smile.

"You can lose the smile. I know what's going through that head of yours. You're thinking that you aren't ever getting rid of me."

"It's crossed my mind a time or two. But, Gramps, I know it's going to be hard for you to step away after thirty-five years in this clinic. In fact, I don't expect you to make a clean break from something you love doing. Gran doesn't either. But with me here, you don't have to worry about the place twenty-four/seven. You can drop in and work whenever you need a fix."

"You think you got your old Gramps pegged, do you?"

"Sorry to interrupt." Ann, one of the clinic's vet techs, stuck her head in before I could answer.

"It's okay, Ann. Here's the Schultz's meds for Bo. That's all they're waiting on."

She stepped around Gramps, and I handed the prescription over to her. When I looked back at Gramps to answer, his brows were furrowed as he looked me over.

"You sure you're doing okay, pumpkin? The last few days you've seemed a little out of sorts."

"I'll be fine. Ann and Candace are here and I'm sure between the three of us, we can close the clinic."

"It's not the clinic I'm worried about. I worry about you. You okay with everything going on? It's not just Ry that's had to adjust having Reed in his life suddenly."

Gramps always could read me. And why I thought I could hide anything from him was beyond me.

"Ry and Reed are just finding their footing with each other. And though they're doing great and getting along, it has been only a week. I don't want to jeopardize what they've accomplished so far, or their future relationship, by getting involved with Reed on a personal level. I mean, what if what is going on with Reed and I is just because of Ry or acting on feelings from the past, then one day realizing it. Ry would be the one hurt. Reagan would be, too, by association.

"Having Reed around every evening this week. Sharing dinner with him. Watching him not only grow closer to Ry but Reagan, too. It's not just my life, Gramps."

Gramps stepped all the way into the room and closed the door. "Raven, do you love, Reed?"

"I don't know. I want him, and I feel his want for me. And in some way, I do love him, but is it because of how he is with the kids? So much is at stake, and I'm afraid one wrong step with Reed will be the end to everything, Gramps."

"He loves you, Raven."

"You can't know that." I looked at the man who essentially raised me. A man who never judged, not once. The only time he voiced disproval with me was over my decision not to tell Reed about Ry. And even though he was against it, he supported me in the end and kept my secret over the years, even living in the town where chances were great that he'd run into Reed.

"No man looks at a woman like Reed looks at you and not be in love with her. Oh, there's want in his eyes, too. But do you think Reed hasn't thought about how what he does with you will affect Ry? I can't tell you how to feel or know what you feel, Raven, but I can tell you what I see and think. And what I think is you are having trouble viewing Reed as a full-grown man and yourself as a woman. Instead, you're looking at him as the nineteen-year-old young man who broke your heart with harsh words. Want some advice?"

"Maybe."

"Stop spending so much time in your head. And I'm not saying you shouldn't think of Ry and Reagan, but you can't put your life on hold for what ifs. Whether you and Reed end up together or you find someone else. If you figure out that you do love him, then don't cheat yourself out of the chance for happiness…you deserve it, Raven, even if you think you don't."

I walked to Gramps and hugged him. "Love you."

"Love you more," he responded, then let me go. "Now get back to work. Someone has to run this place so I can laze around."

"You've never been lazy a day in your life. Are you sure you and Gran don't mind keeping an eye on Ry and Reagan tonight?"

"Not at all. Stop worrying and enjoy yourself—not too much, though. I hear those clubhouse parties get a little rowdy."

"Gramps!"

"What? The MC's been in this town as long as I've been alive. When I was young, it was no secret they were into a few illegal activities. Over the years, I've seen them go from bad to worse. Even if I didn't know any specifics about the club. However, I also watched Reed's dad put in years of work cleaning up Haven after it had been under the reign of his grandfather and dad."

"I'm not sure what the club does or doesn't do. Reed never talks about it. He only talks about his brothers and stuff in general. But I guess I'm going to get a firsthand experience tonight. And I'll admit, I'm a little nervous about going. The men and women are close-knit, and I assume they know about me keeping Ry from Reed. Not sure how accepting of me being there they'll be."

"Give Reed credit, Raven. He wouldn't be taking you there for his buddies and their women to ostracize you."

"I know. I guess I'm just nervous about meeting them."

"Be yourself, Raven, and you'll be just fine."

"Yeah. Thanks for the pep talk, Gramps."

"Anytime, pumpkin. I'm going to go get Sabith from my office and head home."

"Alright. I'll try not to be too late."

"Don't worry about how late you come home." Gramps opened the door and started to leave but paused. "And don't worry if you decide *not* to come home."

"Raven."

I looked up from the computer when I heard Candice whisper my name. I was sitting in the office looking over the upcoming week's surgery calendar.

"Why are you whispering, Candice?"

"Because I don't want the biker from the Haven MC in the waiting area asking for you to hear me. In case you need me to tell him you aren't here."

I leaned forward and whispered back, "Candice, you can send him back. Reed's here to pick me up."

"No shit," Candice said and slapped her hand over mouth. "Oh my God, Raven, I'm sorry. That was rude. It's just you haven't dated since you moved here, and… I'm going to stop rambling now."

I heard a chuckle before the "Excuse me." Then Reed's face popped around the corner. "When no one came to the front after the door chimed, I figured you didn't hear it. Came back to tell you there's a lady at the counter."

Candice rushed out, and Reed stepped into the office.

"You made an impression on the receptionist."

"I heard. Hide from people looking for you?"

"Only tall…" I stood and started walking toward Reed. "…handsome…hot…men," I said the last word when I stopped in front of him.

"Is that so?"

Thinking of Gramps and my talk, I grabbed onto Reed's forearms, then stood on tiptoes and kissed him. He opened his mouth and let me, and the whole time we kissed, he participated without touching me. Letting me take the lead, instead of taking over. I'd never been the aggressor. Maybe it was time to change that.

I ended the kiss and dropped back to my feet. "It will only take me a few minutes to close the clinic, and then I'll be ready."

"Need to stop by my place on the way to the clubhouse."

"Okay, be ready in five. You want to wait in here?"

"No, I'll wait in the truck. And so you know—I like being greeted like that."

As he walked away, I grinned and started shutting down the computer. Just maybe we could make it work.

"Are you sure I'm dressed okay?" I pulled on the bottom of the V-neck sweater I wore with jeans and my boots.

"You look fine, great. I've told you that three times," he said as he opened the door to his house.

"What do the other women wear to these parties?"

"Depends."

"What do you mean depends?"

"Whether they are ol' ladies, hang-arounds, women looking for fun…"

"Well, if I'm not dressed appropriately, you are taking me home."

"Geez, Raven, it isn't a fashion show. It's a biker party. You could show up in a sheet and no one would care."

"I should have brought a change of clothes to work, but I didn't think about it. I hope you can't smell animals on me." I lifted my arm and smelled my sleeve.

Reed laughed and grabbed my arm. "Come on, I want your opinion. I set up Ry's room this week."

"You didn't mention it."

"No, because I wanted you to see it first. If you think he won't like it, I'll switch it out."

"Reed, a bed, maybe a TV, and a place to put his clothes is fine."

He opened the door and we walked into what would be Ry's room when he stayed over at Reed's house.

"Dear God, after he sees this, he won't ever come home. You will be stuck with him."

"Alright, I might have gone a little overboard."

"Is that a mini-fridge?"

"Yeah, that was Train's idea. Nothing sucks when you're in the middle of a game and have to pause it to go to the kitchen and grab a drink."

I had no words for the room. The furniture was fine, it was the amenities that put if over the top. A flat-screen mounted on the wall, a game system with games, a computer on the desk.

"Reed, it's…" I was sincerely at a loss for words.

162

"If you're having problems with this. You probably aren't going to like what else I got."

"There's more?"

"I know it's a lot, but I've missed so much…and I want him to like coming here."

"Oh, Reed. Buying him things. You didn't have to do anything to get Ry to want to spend time with you. Showing him what you have," I laid my hand over his heart, "in here will do it. Spending time with him. Letting him get to know you. And you've gotten a good start on those. You've made time for him every day."

"Thanks, Raven. You've done a good job raising him. He's a great kid. And I enjoyed every minute I spent with him this week."

"I'm glad."

"Well, what the hell am I supposed to do about this room now? Christ, what was I thinking?" He ran his fingers through his hair and then started laughing. "Damn salesman saw my ass coming."

"Yes, he did. You probably made his month in commission."

"I'm giving you a heads up, Raven. If the kid says one smartass thing about this room. I might just drown him in the pool."

"Joking aside, it's an awesome room. Ry will love it. But seriously, take the mini-fridge out."

"Yeah, I will. That really put the room over the top."

"Okay, we'll go with that." I chuckled and then stopped and looked at Reed. "What did you mean by I won't like what else you got?"

"You going to be mad all night?" Reed asked as he took off his helmet. We'd switched the truck for the bike when we left his house.

"I'm not mad. I'm scared he's going to get hurt."

"Raven, are you scared because of how your husband died?"

"It wasn't his first time on an ATV, Reed, and look what happened."

"Do you think I'm going to let Ry take off on the bike without any instructions or supervision? I wanted to get him something special for his thirteen birthday. He'll be officially a teenager. And I got the bike as an early present because we'll still have a few decent days for him to enjoy it before it's too cold. Babe, you can't let your fear transfer to him."

"I know. But he doesn't ride unless you are around to supervise. He has to stay in sight, so if something does happen you'll see it and be able to get to him."

"Deal."

"You don't have any more surprises, do you? Because after seeing the bedroom setup, then you opened the garage door and I saw the dirt bike sitting on the trailer—I'm not sure I can take any more surprises," I said as we reached the door to the clubhouse.

"No more surprises," Reed said, then held the door open for me and I walked inside.

"You're such a liar," I said and stopped in my tracks.

CM Books, LLC

CM Books, LLC

Chapter Thirteen

Keg

I'd held the door open and let Raven walk in ahead me, then stopped so I didn't plow her over.

"You're such a liar," Raven said frozen in her spot.

"Huh?"

"I'm overdressed, and it has nothing to with style. I mean actual items of clothing."

I followed where she was looking and saw Tandy and Ginger, a couple of the regular club girls, talking with the man of the hour, Taylor.

"My clothes are frumpy, and I'm old."

I shook my head at her deadpan response and couldn't help but chuckled.

"It's not funny. If their clothes were any tighter, and I'm being generous referring to them as clothes, they'd need to carry portable oxygen machines to breathe."

CM Books, LLC

I placed my hand at the small of her back. "Your prudish side is kinda cute." That statement earned me what amounted to a death glare.

"I'm not a prude. But hell, my washcloths cover more than that one's top. Her breasts remind me I need to buy a couple cantaloupes when I go to the grocery store."

"They always remind me of the fake fruit my grandmother used to have sitting out. Well, not that big of fruit, but fake nonetheless."

I'd heard the outside door open behind us and given Raven a little nudge to move us out of the way for whoever was coming in. The reply belonged to Charlie, who'd came in and now stood beside Raven looking at Ginger. By the snort that followed Charlie's dig, Hawk was behind me.

"Ripened fruit," Hawk said, and I turned to look at him, shook my head and smirked. He knew saying that shit would set Charlie off. I swear the two of them used it as foreplay.

Raven and Charlie both turned.

"And if I catch you squeezing that fruit, I'm going to cook up some sausage and add a couple of walnuts to it," Charlie said, and even knowing it was a joke, I caught myself adjusting my stance.

Raven's eyes landed on me. I saw the question in them. I wouldn't apologize for anything I've done; it wasn't even up for discussion.

"I haven't been a monk. I'm not going to discuss who I've been with, nothing. If you feel you need to know, I don't

CM Books, LLC

know what to tell 'cause my answer will be 'no comment' if you ask."

"That pretty much means you have slept with her." Raven looked over her shoulder. "Or them," she said snidely and maybe coated with a little jealously.

Which was interesting, and I'll admit a tad pleasing. I'd been pushing her this past week. Kissing her goodbye when I left. Touching her when she'd been close. I'd spent time getting to know my son, but I took advantage of Raven being there, too. I needed to know if what I was feeling for her was real or just because she and I shared Ry between us. I never took it past kissing and small touches, and I knew I was getting to her and testing my own restraints because I'd leave wanting nothing more than to throw her over my shoulder and take her with me.

"No comment," I answered. She'd have to be able to accept the club, the guys, even the club girls and hang-arounds. If she wasn't going to try, then regardless of what I was feeling for her, there really wasn't a reason to get involved. We'd both have to have trust in each other. "If you've changed your mind about being here, I'll take you home and come back," I said, placing the ball so to speak in her court.

"It—"

"Charlie," Hawk cut Charlie off before she could put her two cents in. He understood what was happening.

Raven would stay, and we'd both move to the next level in a relationship. Or she'd ask to be taken home and

169

we'd both move on and only deal with each other when it concerned Ry. I stared at her and waited.

"Wow, what is it with this place?" She looked over at Charlie as she asked.

I could physically feel the resolve settling in along with disappoint that Raven wasn't going to be able to accept all parts of my life. I glanced at Hawk and received a silent 'sorry, brother' look in return.

"Is it just Reed, or all of them, that their arrogance magically switches on when they cross the entrance?"

My lips twitched, and I noticed Hawk's did, too. And Charlie, being Charlie, went with the flow.

"Girl, tell me about it. I think arrogance is a prerequisite to becoming a member of the club. You'd think I would be used to it, but no, one of them says or does something and bam, I'm shocked." Hawk and I watched as Charlie put her arm through Raven's and started leading her away. "Come on, I'm starved, and the spread of food is in the kitchen. It's where we'll find the other women. I'm Charlie if you didn't catch it before, and the lug I'm with is Hawk, or Kaden, whatever you want to call him. He's the VP, vice president of Haven MC."

I looked over at Hawk as we followed the women, listening to Charlie. "Still not referring to herself as your ol' lady?"

Hawk chuckled. "I call her it when I really want to get under her skin. She knows she is, and she knows it is a term we use for *the* woman in our life, but she swears it's archaic and cavemanish, and that last one is her word."

CM Books, LLC

"What term does she think should be used?"

"I don't know. And I'm not asking. I asked if she liked ball and chain better—and for a week, brother, I had to hide her damn taser and sleep with one eye open. Crazy ass woman."

"But she's your woman."

"Damn straight." He lifted his chin at the women, then added, "At least you aren't going to have to spend your evening with introductions and who's who, Charlie will have it all taken care of for you before the evening is over. You looking to head into ol' lady territory with Raven? If you're not, I'll tell Charlie to cool it with the Introduction to Haven MC 101."

"A little late for that," I said as we walked into the kitchen, and Charlie started immediately introducing Raven to everyone. Thank God the kitchen was huge. At the oversized table sat my dad, Moose and Katie, Smoke and Tink, Fire and Macy, Tram, and Roach. But the ones at the table that caught me by surprise was Shock and Freak.

The two kept getting more and more social, and that started with Katie and Charlie.

I looked over at the food lined on the counter and island, buffet style, and found Pinch and Crank working their way around it, loading their plates.

"How's baby's momma?" Crank said and made a motion with his head in Raven's direction.

"Good one, brother," Pinch said and patted Crank on the back.

"Really, man." I snorted. "Raven's fine."

171

"You could do worse," Hawk said, then chuckled. "And you have." The three of them laughed.

"Fuck all three of you." I started placing food on two plates.

"You know, it's probably good you never brought her around the club before," Pinch said.

"Dumbass, she and I were in high school back then. And none of you were even in the club yet."

"You were still dating her when we were all prospecting," Crank said and leaned against the counter and started eating from his plate.

"She was sixteen when *I* started prospecting. She was too young to be at the clubhouse or near it."

"Brother, back then, I don't think some of the brothers would have cared about her age or that she was yours," Pinch said, then shrugged when I looked at him.

What Pinch said placed a new light on things for me. I'd never brought Raven to the clubhouse, not even when there were cookouts when the family and girlfriends could attend. I'd come with my dad and Sami, then go see Raven afterward.

Between the weed, booze, and other drugs some of the guys were using, they wouldn't have given a shit about her age. Dad had kept Sami in his sights every time we were at the clubhouse. If he had to go to meet in his office with someone, he'd tell me to glue myself to her. And she'd been called princess since the day we moved there.

Raven wouldn't have had the advantage of being the president's daughter. They hadn't messed with Sami because they knew Wild Bill. They would have paid with their life if they had.

They would have taken Raven as a challenge to me. The son of the president. Stone and his followers never liked me from day one. Even though I was just a kid. And as I stood there with two filled plates, I found I was thankful I hadn't known about Ry because Raven and he would have been targets. Like Sami, I would have had no choice but to hide them away when Stone went in the wind. I wouldn't have put it past the asshole to have taken her in his little trafficking deal with Kosnoff.

Finding I had a son and that I missed those years hurt, but how bad would it have hurt to have known him, then have to send him away or worse, he'd been hurt himself or killed as a distraction. A distraction to take Wild Bill's focus off cleaning up Haven, and Stone would have taken any advantage he could to gain the seat of the president.

Yeah, that shit was an eye opener. I might not have known Ry existed then, but he'd been safe and away from the crap Haven had gone through. That counted as a big thing in my book and eased a little more of my hurt.

"Reed?"

"Yeah," I automatically answered and was pulled from my thoughts to find Raven beside me.

"I could have fixed my own plate."

I looked down at the plates in my hand, then handed one to her. "You were meeting everyone over at the table. You've met Pinch, his real name's Cal. The one leaning on the counter is Merit, who goes by Crank. Hawk, you met. This is Raven, Ry's mom."

They greeted Raven, and she spoke to each man, then we went to the table and sat down with the others to eat.

Conversation flowed around the table, and Raven participated as though she'd known everyone forever.

"Frankie and Steven are going to volunteer some of their time at the shelter. They always can use help with walking dogs or just spending time with the animals. The shelter employees aren't left with much time to allow one on one with the dogs and cats after cleaning up, watering and feeding them," Raven said and smiled at Shock and Freak who sat across from us.

"Did you come with me tonight to recruit helpers for the shelter?" She slapped my arm, and I laughed.

"No!" she said, then looked around the table. "Oh my God, I hope you all don't think that."

My dad smiled. "Sweetheart, no one thinks that. Hell, helping with the animals could be healing for some of us." Dad looked over at Shock and Freak, then at me. Raven didn't know what he was talking about, but I did. Shock and Freak were venturing outside Haven when last year they barely came out of the basement to eat. And there was no way to deny it was because of the women we were bringing into the mix. The women not only didn't avoid them, they interacted with them. Even included them in things, leaving it up to them if they came to a cookout or dinner at one of their homes.

"Does the shelter here have a lot of animals waiting for homes?" Tram asked.

"They are always at capacity. But with the help of fosters and rescues, they're able to find homes, which frees up place for more. It's a never-ending cycle. I hate going there because I want to take them all home."

"Reagan wants a dog. Why don't you get her one from there?" I brought up.

"I'm planning to get her a dog and yes, from the shelter, after I find us a place to live. If Hope is still at the shelter, I'm going to adopt her."

"Hope?" I asked and furrowed my brows.

"She's a black lab that was picked up as a stray. She was in bad shape Aline, the shelter manager, told me when I asked about her. Every time I go there, she's there, and I promised myself if she was still there when I found a house, I would adopt her. I estimate her to be about five or six, and she's been at the shelter the longest, four hundred days."

"How come no one wants to adopt her? Or foster her? She's a lab, why didn't a rescue take her?" Tram pressed.

"Well, Aline said she gets passed over because she only has one ear. They don't know what happened, but best guess is she got in a fight while running loose. When they picked her up, the ear was pretty chewed up, and Gramps is the one who did the surgery to remove the flap because infection was setting up in the wound. None of the fosters can take her because they have more dogs or cats in their care and Hope needs to be an only pet. Guess running loose and being on her own and fighting to eat, soured the poor girl on other animals. Her not getting along with other animals is also why I didn't bring her to Gramps. He has Sabith who is older, and it wouldn't be fair to her or Hope if we had to quarantine them from each other."

"What about a rescue?" I repeated Tram's question.

"They'd pull her if the shelter here was a kill shelter. But since it isn't, she's safe and fed until she finds a forever home. Labs, retriever breeds period, are in abundance in shelters, and the number put down a year across this country saddens me. The breed ranks one of the highest in animals euthanized."

"If she was a stray, how'd they know her name was Hope?" Tram asked.

"They're given names in the shelter if they don't have one because they don't know how long they will be there and it's good for the animals. Aline started calling her Hope on the third day she was in the shelter and people kept passing her over. Hope for 'hope' someone adopts her."

"Damn, woman, you know how to bring down a room," Moose said.

"I'm sorry. I didn't mean to make everyone feel bad. I'm a vet because I love animals, which makes me passionate about them all."

Tram pushed back his chair and stood, he said, "Getting a drink and congratulating Taylor." He tossed his paper plate in the trash, and as he went to pass the table on his way out of the kitchen, he stopped by Raven's chair. "I know you were going to adopt the dog when you got a place, but she needs one now. I'll go by the shelter Monday," he said and walked out, not waiting for a reply.

"We're going next week, too, and look," Katie said, and her and Moose stood and left the kitchen.

"Screw it. We already have three dogs. What's one more," Smoke said.

"Yeah, we got two. Another won't be a big deal," Fire said, and he and Macy, and Smoke and Tink left the table.

"Well, shit. We're going to the shelter, too, Kaden. That's sad. There's probably a dog there waiting for us to come to take it home," Charlie said, stood, and grabbed both her and Hawk's plates.

Hawk pointed at Raven when Charlie walked off to throw the plates away. "I'm holding you responsible if she adopts a big motherfucker that chews my shit," he said and led Charlie out of the kitchen with Crank and Pinch on their heels. I didn't miss they didn't comment, they just escaped.

Shock and Freak were the next to push away from the table, and both had small grins on their faces, which was alarming.

"We're heading downstairs. Raven, it was good seeing you again. Don't be a stranger," Shock said, and I glanced at my dad, and he shrugged.

"Looking forward to helping out at the shelter. Thanks for bringing it up. Maybe I'll even find an animal who needs an old man like me," Freak said, and he and Shock headed to the basement.

I looked around the kitchen. "Babe, you sure can clear a room."

My dad laughed and stood. "I wonder what the shelter's going to think of their boost in adoptions?"

"I wouldn't have said... Oh, never mind. I'm just sorry I ran everyone off."

"Club is called Haven," I said, leaned over and kissed her head, then rose to discard our plates.

"Yes, it is." My dad tossed his plate in the can.

"You were about the only one at the table that isn't running to the shelter." I chuckled.

"What makes you think I'm not? Gets lonely in that house sometimes," he said and walked out.

"Come on, babe. Let's go into the party and help Taylor celebrate."

"That's if everyone doesn't run out of the room when I enter," she said as we made our way to the main room.

"It's a good possibility." She poked me in the stomach, and I grabbed her hand and lifted it up and kissed it. "Just so you know—you're coming home with me tonight."

"I thought you'd never ask."

I pushed her body against the door.

She yanked my shirt out from the waist of my pants.

I shoved my hands in her hair and jerked her head back.

She slid her hands under my shirt and up my chest, using her nails to leave a trail of fire.

I bit her lips.

She bit mine back.

I forced my tongue between her lips.

She sucked it in.

Every move calculated.

Every touch like a splash of gasoline on an already burning fire.

I broke the kiss and rested my forehead against hers.

"You know we've been leading up to this for a week. For every kiss and touch I gave you, it cost me when I left alone. So fair warning, I'm not sure I can go slow or even be gentle with you this first round. But for you, I'll try." I leaned down and met her lips again. I ran the tip of my tongue lazily over the seam. Raven's taste was intoxicating as it exploded on my tongue. I sucked her bottom lip between my teeth and bit down. When she gasped, I pushed my tongue in, and her taste mixed with mine as I explored every crevice. I kissed her long and hard, and when I broke the kiss, I buried my face between her neck and shoulder and fought for my breath.

Raven's breaths came just as hard. Her breasts rising with each one she took, and it brought her breasts close enough to graze my chest.

"Please, Reed, take me."

Her words. Her scent. Her taste. All three overloaded my senses. The effect had me trailing kisses and nips down her neck, across her collarbone and down until I reached her covered breasts. I wanted no barriers between us. I needed to feel her skin against mine.

Grabbing her by the waist, I lifted, and she wrapped her legs around me. In my bedroom, I let her body slide easily from mine until her feet were planted on the floor. I could feel my control slipping and, reaching for the bottom of her sweater, I lifted it up and over her head. Once I removed her bra, I leaned down and ran my tongue around her taut nipple, biting down gently, using the tip of my tongue to soothe any sting away. Showing her other breast the same attention.

Raven moaned her displeasure as I pulled away, leaving her wet, taut nipple in the open air of the room. I quickly discarded my clothes, then standing naked, I watched her eyes roam over my body. Feeling the trail of fire burning down my spine, taking my breath.

I dropped to my knees, lifted her leg and pulled the boot from her foot, then moved to the other foot and did the same. At her waist, I unsnapped her jeans, slowly sliding the zipper. The anticipation of having Raven naked standing before me was almost too much.

Sliding the jeans over her hips and down her legs, I left them to pool on the floor. A tiny triangle of lace blocked what was mine. Reaching for it, I held the edge, and with one quick snap of the wrist, the lacy floated to the ground.

The changes in her body from the young girl to the woman only enhanced her beauty. Her breasts soft yet heavy to the touch. The faint lines between her hips left from carrying Ry and Reagan. Hips that flared from her waist.

Her body called to me.

I leaned forward until my face was buried at her mound. The smell of her arousal filling my nostrils. I grabbed the back of one knee and lifted, holding it at my

180

shoulder. One swipe of my tongue through her folds snapped my control.

Placing her foot back on the ground, I rose from my knees and scooped her up in my arms and carried her to the bed.

CM Books, LLC

CM Books, LLC

Chapter Fourteen

Raven

A week of foreplay. A bike ride holding onto him, pressed against him. The heat between our bodies, the vibration of the bike between my legs, intensified everything. A blaze burned in my center from the anticipation of what was to come.

Pulling into the garage, my heart raced faster, and the steps to the door was made on trembling legs. An echo of a click was heard as the door shut, leaving me with the scent of Reed surrounding me.

He pushed my body against the door.

I yanked his shirt out from the waist of his pants.

He shoved his hands in my hair and jerked my head back.

I slid my hands under his shirt and up his chest, using my nails to leave a trail as they scorched his skin.

He bit my lips.

I bit his back.

183

He forced his tongue between my lips.

I sucked it in.

Reed lifted me and carried me to his bedroom, his slow removal of my clothes as he took his time suckling my breasts.

When he stripped and stood before me naked, I felt the quiver in my stomach, a weakness in my knees. He was perfection and mine. His body was familiar yet different.

The swipe of his tongue through my folds undid me. And time meant nothing. Only him. Through my eyes, I let the young boy I'd known fade and welcome the man he became.

When he abruptly stopped and dropped my leg then picked me up and carried me to his bed, I wasn't sure I would survive this man's attention. He laid me on his bed and followed me down, and I felt his cock throb between us. He shifted and started a journey down my body, kissing my skin along the way.

He worked his way down my body that held the changes motherhood had brought. As he reached my mound, I reached for him, weaving my fingers in his hair, trying to guide him where the flame burned.

Reed slid his hands over my body until he reached my thighs, then he spread me wide. He didn't hesitate. With his tongue, he licked me from back to front. Each swipe bringing more wetness from my center.

My moans the only sounds in the room until his tongue pierced my entrance. I arched my back and dug my nails in his scalp. And I screamed, "Reed!" when he moved his tongue from my entrance and placed it against my swollen nub.

When he circled the nub with the tip of his tongue and then sucked while he pushed a finger inside me, my thighs trembled, and my orgasm was just out of reach.

"More, please, Reed. I need more."

He added a finger into my depths and pumped them in and out. When he bit down gently on my clit, my body spasmed as my orgasm exploded. Using his fingers, he helped me ride out the tremors until my body went lax.

Moving back up my body, he reached my lips, and I opened, allowing him entrance. He broke the kiss and lifted, holding his weight on one arm and grasping his cock with other.

"Fuck! I got to grab a condom."

I tightened my hold on his back, stopping him. "I'm on the pill."

"Raven, I've always used a condom, are you sure?" he asked, poised at my entrance.

"Yes," was barely out of my mouth, and he was pushing against my entrance.

I felt pressure as he worked inch by inch to fill me.

"Christ, you're tight," he said through gritted teeth.

Once he was into the hilt, he paused giving me time to adjust.

"Not sure how long I'll last," he said and pulled back before thrusting back in.

I lifted my hips to meet his thrusts, and Reed set a pace that had us both on the brink.

"God, Reed," I said as the orgasm consumed me.

Reed hiked up one of my legs, and as my body shook from my release, he rode my wave, filling me to hilt each time, taking what he needed for his own release. When he stiffened, I felt the warmth of his release as it spilled inside me.

When our bodies and breathing settled, he pulled out and fell to my side, pulling me into his arms.

As we laid there catching our breath, something Reed said registered in my head.

"Reed?"

"Hmmm."

"There were a few times you didn't wear a condom. We have living proof."

The smack on my butt stung. "You're so cute when you're being a smartass. I'll correct that statement to I've never went without a condom after you. Better?"

"We could be the poster couple for pulling out doesn't always work either."

"Stop, woman, I'm trying to get enough energy so we can have round two. You drained me."

"Let me know when you get the energy. I'll just be here taking a little nap," I said on a yawn and closed my eyes. The pinch on my butt made me smile.

I'd forgotten how good morning sex was. I pulled my jeans up, and when the seam hit between my legs, it instantly reminded me that until last night, I hadn't had sex in a year.

186

I walked out of the bathroom and into the bedroom. "You sore?" Reed asked as he walked in carrying a cup, and the aroma of coffee hit my nose.

"A little. It would've been better if I'd had underwear to put on."

He handed over the coffee. "You could've put a pair of my boxers on."

"I think I can survive until I get home."

"You sure you don't mind me hanging around today?"

"I know you are excited to give Ry the bike. Just be prepared because your day will be spent teaching him to ride. And, Reed?"

"I won't let him get hurt, Raven. Trust me?"

"Yes. But I'll just stay in the house anyway and help Gran. I'm not sure I can watch." I walked out of the bedroom and into the kitchen and placed the coffee cup in the sink. "Ready when you are."

"I already hooked the trailer to the truck and pulled it out of the garage. We can go out the front."

"Okay."

After walking out of the house, we got in the truck and were on our way.

"I can't do what we did last night again," I said, turning to face Reed.

He glanced in my direction and back to the road. "Ever?"

I chuckled. "You know what I mean. I can't leave the kids with Gran and Gramps to have sex with you. It will confuse the kids. And I don't want what this is," I waved my hand between him and me, "between us, messing anything up between you and Ry."

"I don't want that either, Rav, but we are allowed to take some time for ourselves to explore this. And Ry and I will be fine."

"Okay, but what time are you suggesting, Reed? You have club business, I work, and you spend the afternoon and evening with Ry, which needs to stay that way. So I'm not seeing much free time for us to sneak a few minutes."

"First off, woman, you wound me—a few minutes? It takes that long to heat you up."

I reached over and smacked his leg. "Stop it, this is serious."

Reed sighed, then said, "I know, Rav. I'm flexible with time unless I have to attend a meeting, so what about you?"

"We close the clinic for an hour and a half for lunch from twelve to one thirty. It closes at five, but sometimes we go over if we get backed up during the day. So, I am left with evenings. And that's your time with Ry."

"We can work with that. Lunchtime rendezvous and the occasional dinner date with no sleeping over."

We turned and started up the driveway to my grandparents' house. "Awesome, we reverted back to teenagers."

Reed chuckled. "Yes, but this time around we have a place where we can be alone and have no worry that someone could be walking in at any time."

"Fine, when do you want to start to have our secret little meetings?"

CM Books, LLC

"Monday. I'll meet you at my house at twelve," he said and parked the truck on the side of the garage out of the way with the trailer hitched.

We got out of the truck, and I heard the front door open. Ry stepped out of the house, followed by Gran, Gramps, and Reagan. Ry's eye went to Reed as he dropped the gate on the trailer.

Reed had strapped down a tarp over the bike, and unless someone looked closely, they wouldn't be able to tell what kind of bike, just that it was one.

"Why you pulling your bike? Is it broken down?" Ry asked as he walked toward Reed.

"No, bike's good. Help me pull this thing off, buddy," Reed said, and Ry jumped up in the trailer.

"You and Mom going riding today?"

I stood there watching father and son work together to unmask the bike. When Ry asked if Reed was taking me riding, I smiled because Ry was more interested in why the bike was on the trailer than why his mother stayed out all night.

"What did you and Reed do for your sleepover? Did you make popcorn and hot chocolate and watch movies like we do?"

I looked at Gran and Gramps, and they were trying to cover up their grins. Reed snorted, and Ry shook his head. I'd had *the* talk with Ry, so it wasn't a stretch to think he knew what his mom and dad were up to. I wasn't bringing it up, but his no big deal attitude about Reed and me came as a surprise.

CM Books, LLC

"Yep, and we watched a scary movie," I lied, then glared as Reed snorted again.

Reagan's nose crinkled. "I don't like scary movies," she said and moved closer to the trailer where the last of the tie off straps were being undone.

"I think it's bothering you more than them. They're fine, Raven. Stop worrying," Gramps whispered as he stepped up beside me.

"Is what I think under that cover?" Gran asked in a low voice.

"Yes," I said and sighed, and Gran wrapped her arm around my waist and squeezed my side.

Reed grabbed one edge of the tarp. "Normally, you fold these things as you go, so they aren't a pain in the ass when it's put back on. Today's an exception." Reed yanked on the tarp and the dirt bike came into view.

Ry's eyes widened, but that was the only movement from him as he stood there staring at the bike. We all waited for him to find his voice.

"Is it mine?" he asked and turned to Reed.

"It's an early birthday present," Reed finished. Ry moved to Reed and hugged his waist. It was the first time Ry had initiated any physical contact with Reed.

It took Reed a second to get his voice back when they broke apart. "Got rules I expect followed, or you can kiss that bike goodbye, hear me?"

"Yes, sir."

"Then let's get this thing unloaded and get started."

CM Books, LLC

Ry whooped, then he and Reed worked getting the bike off the trailer.

"So, can I have a dog now?"

I put my arm on Reagan's shoulder. "It will be the first thing we do after we get into our own place, okay?"

"Okay, but I get to pick it out."

"You got it, sweetie."

"Ry's gotten that down," Gran said, looking out the window as she stood beside me at the sink where I was washing the dishes from the early Sunday meal. When Gran heard Reed mention earlier in the week he wouldn't be able to stay as long Sunday, she switched the big meal to a late lunch and said we could pick on leftovers that night if we got hungry. Gramps had given Gran a look, and she started going on about Reed needing to eat, too.

"Ry has done good on the bike. But it's been the longest week of my life. Those first few days were rough on me to watch him."

"I know, sweetie. You did good. I went past a window the other day and glanced out in time to see the bike shoot forward right out from under Ry. I thought for sure with how hard he hit the ground he'd broken his tailbone," Gran said, and I nodded in agreement.

The week had seemed long in one aspect and short in another. Alone time for Reed and I would fly by. I wanted more, but Ry came first. Watching Ry learn to ride the dirt bike, stripped my nerves raw. I didn't want to be that mom, so I stayed inside and watched from the windows.

191

Reed had been patient with Ry as he instructed him. Ry listened to everything Reed said with admiration for him. If I'd been worried about the acceptance for one another, it went away with watching them interact. After Reed would leave and head home, Ry would talk about him. Reed said this. Reed said I had to do that. I was getting to witness their father/son bond grow.

"Reed's good with Ry. He's also good with Reagan."

It was close to the time Reed said he had to leave. Ry stopped the bike and swapped places with Reed. After Reed straddled the bike, Reagan climbed on in front of him, and I smiled watching Ry place his helmet on her head, then tap the top.

Reed always gave her a ride around the property after Ry's lesson was over. Gran was right, he was good with her.

"He always includes her. It doesn't matter what he and Ry are doing," I said because Reed had been doing it from the beginning with Reagan when he didn't have to. She wasn't his responsibility.

Reed pulled up to the back porch and helped Reagan off the bike. A smile stretched across her face as she looked at Reed.

I went to the back door as Reed started for the stairs while Ry began rolling the bike around the side of the house. Reagan followed Ry carrying his helmet.

"Ry's putting the bike up. I'll check on him when I go to get on my bike. Wanted to tell you goodbye and get my kiss before I headed out."

"Is that so?"

192

"Yeah. Come here." He grabbed my waist and gave a tug until I stood flush against him. "Don't forget our lunch date tomorrow."

"I won't. I'll meet you at your house with bells on."

He chuckled and bent his head, and I stretched to meet him when Ry's words reached us from the side of the garage and the moment ended.

"Reagan! Don't go near it. It's hurt and might bite you."

Reed let go of me and was off the porch and breaking into jog before I had made it down the steps. I ran, but his long legs already had him turning the corner of the house.

"Reagan, get away from the dog!" Reed yelled, and panic struck me.

I made it to the end of the house and came to a stop. Reagan was sitting on the ground with a strange dog laid out beside her, its head in her lap. The dog looked like a pit/mastiff mix. I noticed dried blood in its fur and at least two open wounds on its body, and that it was underweight.

Reed stood behind Reagan ready to snatch her up if the animal made a wrong move.

Ry stood in front of the bike that laid on the ground.

"Reagan, you know better than to touch strange animals, especially ones that are hurt. They're unpredictable." I moved to Reagan slowly so I wouldn't startle the dog. Once at her side, I squatted beside her.

"It's okay. I won't hurt you. My mommy can help you, she's an animal doctor," Reagan talked to the animal and petted its head. It even cocked its head a little as if it listened to her.

"Reagan, you need to get out from under him, so I can examine him. Ry, go get Gramps and tell him to bring one of the spare leashes and a blanket."

"I want to keep him, Mommy. He came to me because he needs me."

"Ry? Did you see what direction it came from?" Reed asked.

"It came out of the woods, right there." Ry pointed to the area at the tree line. "Before I could set the bike down, Reagan was approaching it. It hasn't growled or anything. She sat on the ground, and it laid down, too, then put its head in her lap."

"Okay. Go get your Gramps, like your mother asked," Reed said, then squatted beside me, looking the dog over.

Ry started to go around the house and stopped. "Oh, before the dog came out of the woods, I heard a man yelling, but I couldn't understand what he said."

"From the woods?" Reed asked.

"I guess. He sounded far away. That's why I couldn't make out what he was yelling." Ry left to go get Gramps, and I started assessing the dog's wounds while it continued to lay still with Reagan petting him.

"Hmm, it's got a piece of rope around its neck, the edge is snapped off. Looks like he broke free and took off."

"Maybe he belongs to the neighbor. Who lives on the other side of the woods?"

194

"Mrs. Jenson used to live there. She died about a year ago Gramps told me. The house and property are tied up because the only relative is a great-grandson, and they're still trying to locate him. There's back taxes owed and some other legal issues with the place. So I don't think the poor thing lived there. Once Gramps gets here, we're going to have to take him to the clinic. Clean out those wounds and see if he has anything else wrong with him. I don't know for sure, but the place on his face looks like a bite, and when he tried to get away from whatever attacked him, the skin tore. The one on his shoulder looks the same."

Reed stood and walked to the edge of the woods and looked around. "Ry said he heard some yelling coming from over there. I'll swing by there when I leave and check it out." Reed walked backed and picked the dirt bike up and leaned it against the house.

"Reed, I thought you had a meeting at the clubhouse? You're going to be late."

"Yeah, I do. But I'm not leaving you here to take care of this. I'll text Dad and tell him I'll be late. I'll help you get the dog loaded to take to the clinic, then I'll head out and swing by the place next door."

"Okay. Will you call me or text me whether you find something or not?"

"Sure."

"Mommy, once you fix him up, can I keep him?"

"Baby, he looks like he belongs to someone because he's been tied up."

"Well, they didn't take good care of him. I would."

195

I looked up at Reed, and his brows lifted. "She's got a point."

"I know, but you can't just take someone's pet, even a mistreated one. You have to go through the channels unless you can get the owner to surrender them."

Reed looked down at Reagan as she whispered to the injured dog, then his eyes went to the dog. "If there is an owner, I'm going to have a little talk with them."

From the look on Reed's face, I wondered if there'd be any talking involved.

CM Books, LLC

Chapter Fifteen

Keg

I helped Raven and her grandfather load the dog in Doc's truck. The kids were staying with her grandmother, to the protest of Reagan, who wanted to go with them. Halo, the name she'd tagged the dog with, needed her. When I asked why that name, she pointedly told me because he was an angel and angels have halos. Kid logic was definitely going to take work on my part.

Reagan was set on keeping the dog, and I was set on seeing that she did. It might be years away, but I had no doubt Reagan would follow in her mother's, her dad's, and her great-grandfather's shoes. Just like I knew, Ry would one day be a part of Haven. Sometimes you just need to trust your gut.

After Raven and Doc pulled out, I mounted my bike and called my dad and told him I'd be there as soon as I stopped at the place next door and checked it out.

I turned into the driveway and made my way up to the house. Like Raven's grandfather's place, it sat a nice bit from the main road. The difference was the house was ranch style and old. I didn't have to stand in front of the place to know it needed a shit ton of work.

I stopped my bike in front and got off, going to the front door. It had a padlock on it, and several different notices slapped on the door. I didn't bother to read them. Instead, I stepped off the porch and went to my bike and retrieved my gun out of the saddlebag. Something felt off so better safe than sorry. I started walking around the house, the backyard was open with a few trees scattered, and the property that surrounded it seemed okay with nothing out of place. I saw an outbuilding in the distance, the type used to store farm equipment. If it belonged to the house, I pegged the property to be close to fifteen acres. If the great-grandson weren't found, the state would end up with it and sell it off for taxes owed. Prime land for some big real estate company to sweep up and build a new housing development.

Movement had me squinting, and I shifted behind a tree. Then I cursed under my breath and pulled out my cell phone.

"What the hell is taking you so long? We're waiting on you," my dad bellowed in my ear. He'd be yelling louder once I told him what I'd seen.

"I'm leaning on a tree in the backyard of the property next to Doc's place."

"Are you fucking kidding me? Get your ass to the clubhouse."

198

"We might want to hold Church here."

"Damn it, has your ass been drinking?"

I heard Moose's voice in the background as he bitched.

"Not a drop. And I have perfect vision."

"Quit dicking around. We need to discuss the Widows and figure out where the hell they are. So if you'd join us, we could get this shit over with."

"I at least know where one of them is."

"You spotted one of the Widows. Wait, you said you're at the property next to Doc's?"

"Yeah. He's at the back end of the property holed up in an outbuilding. Could be more inside, but I laid eyes on the one."

"Guess we know why they haven't been spotted in town."

"There are no vehicles here. And none in front of the outbuilding I'm looking at unless they're pulled around back of it."

"Hell, stay put and out of sight in case more of those assholes are inside. I'm surprised they didn't hear your bike."

"Don't know. Depending on the building, it could be can't hear when you're inside."

"I'm going to call the Chief. I'll get back to you."

I hit the button on my phone and slipped it back in my vest pocket. I wanted to move my bike out of sight in case more Widows showed up. But if I saw movement, they would, too. I also couldn't believe they'd been that close.

Christ, I'd come to Doc's place every day for the last two weeks.

My phone vibrated and pulled it out. "Yeah."

"Me and the boys will be there soon. Will stash the bikes somewhere close and walk in. They might not have heard a single bike, but no way will they not hear a group."

"Only you six coming?"

"No, Shock and Freak are with us."

"Do I want to know?"

"Some things just can't be answered. They're coming in the van."

"Well, with Shock and Freak, it will be interesting if nothing else. Especially with the Chief and some of his guys."

"They'll be behind us. Asked for us to keep watch and make sure the Widows didn't split before he assembled his officers and got out there."

"Fucking awesome."

Dad chuckled. "See you shortly," he said and disconnected. I leaned against the tree and waited, watching the area and wondered how the dog Raven and Doc took to the clinic was doing.

The whistle I heard let me know the brothers were close. If I focused on each sound and separated them, I faintly made out footsteps. Sometimes it bothered me that I was one of the few members of the club who'd never been in the military. The only one who had zilch military training that sat at the table. It wasn't often, but there were times I'd felt like they shared a deeper connection with each other because of the military. Then I'd see Freak and Shock have episodes where they thought they were back in Vietnam and Roach sitting staring at nothing. I'd even walked in my dad's house and found him sleeping on the couch caught in a nightmare.

So yeah, they shared a deeper connection, but to have it, you had to deal with PTSD, and I'd pass—life was hard enough without it. And I had nothing but respect for the strength they had to fight that shit every day.

"Wonder what the inside of the house looks like?" Tram said as they came into view.

"Anything like the outside and demolition is a better option," Pinch said, then he took the spot on the other side of the tree from me. "Spot any more?"

"No, and the one went back inside and hasn't come out again."

"Why don't we do a little recon around the building? Can't hear shit this far away," Moose suggested. I agreed with him. I'd thought about it while I waited, and nothing was going on around the outside of the building.

"Not our show. We are only on standby with the cops," Dad said, looking toward the driveway. "And it looks like the wait for them is over."

The Chief didn't even bother staying out of sight. He drove his cruiser to where we were standing and rolled down the window. The other two police vehicles headed toward the outbuilding.

"What do you got?" Dad stepped up to the vehicle in president mode.

"Had my people run this property and see what they could dig up. Before we pulled out, they had the information. Mrs. Jenson, the old lady who lived here, had/has a great-grandson they've been looking for. Thaddius Jenson." Chief paused and waited.

"Thaddius Jones runs this crew and goes by T-bone. Are you telling me his real name is Jenson?"

"You get the prize, Wild Bill. It seems if you search for Thaddius Jones, nothing connects him to Mrs. Jenson. He must have cared about the woman; he was really careful not to have her tied to the Widows. Running the property and Mrs. Jenson, the owner, well… Thaddius went into foster care after his mom died from an overdose because Mrs. Jenson was already too old and had medical issues, she had to sign off as his only relative. It looks like he took the last name of Jones from the first foster family he had. He built his life off the last name of Jones when he aged out of the system. Everything: social security number, driver's license and bank account." Chief shrugged. "My people are still digging, but that's what they've came up with so far."

"The paper the grandmother signed, it would have been in the system and tagged Thaddius Jenson. Once in that file, there'd be a list of every foster home he was in, which should have brought up Thaddius Jenson being in the care of the Joneses in the first place. And if nothing was in the file. How did you find the information?" Tram asked, and the Chief stared.

"Because the information was just recently added. The older years are still being put in the computer system. The paper with Mrs. Jenson's signature was uploaded five days ago. It's what's known as different office's communication breakdowns and people dropping the ball. Unfortunately, it doesn't happen often, but people do get lost in the system."

"So you think T-Bone is in the building?" I asked, but the Chief didn't get a chance to respond because his radio went off.

"Chief, we grabbed two Widows going out the back. Building is clear, but we're going to need animal control out here."

I barely made out what the officer said because of a dog barking and snarling in the background.

"On my way."

"Wait, I want to go down to the building. The reason I came over here to check is because a dog showed up at the property on the other side of those woods. It was hurt and looked to have broken free by snapping the rope he was tied up with. My woman's a vet and thought the wounds the dog sustained were caused by bites. She thought wild animal or even another dog." The dog suddenly showing up made sense, and even Ry said he heard someone yelling. If they had the dog tied up and it broke free, they could have been yelling for it to come back.

"I don't see a problem with it. You helped us locate at least two of the Widows. They went underground for a reason, so hopefully, we can get the two to share some information."

"There are ways to get that, but…"

The Chief chuckled. "Yes, there are. But I'm not sure the higher-ups would go for that. Not the way the media coverage is all over us if we sneeze wrong while making an arrest."

"We'll get our bikes and meet you at the building, Chief," Wild Bill said, and the Chief saluted and drove away.

"Could this have been any more uneventful?" Hawk said, and I shook my head as we started around the house.

"Looking for excitement, VP? Go to work with your woman," Crank said, and Hawk groaned.

"My luck, Charlie would taser me instead of the skipper. So that would be a big fucking no."

"I'm going to head to the building since I don't have to walk to get my bike," I said and received several fingers as the others kept walking. They'd left the bikes and van pulled off the road in the trees with Latch staying back with them. The prospect had driven the van with Shock and Freak riding with him.

Once I was on my bike, I rode it down to the building. The closer I got, the dog's barking grew louder. I walked around the building and stopped. They had both men cuffed and sitting on the ground while an officer asked them questions. I couldn't hear a word being said for the dog inside.

I walked toward the Chief, who was talking with another officer at the tree line. He turned when he heard me approach. "You don't want to see this shit. I sure could have done without it."

CM Books, LLC

When I looked in the direction of the woods, I felt my stomach turn over.

"Is that what I think it is?" Moose asked as the others walked up.

I turned so my back was to the woods. "Bait animal corpses. Sick fucking bastards." I thought of Reagan naming the dog Halo. She'd been on the mark with that name. 'Cause the dog angels had been watching over him. No doubt he'd escaped from here.

I turned to the Chief. "Have they added dogfighting as a new business venture?" My dad put a hand on my shoulder.

"Keg."

I looked over my shoulder. "I watched Reagan whisper to a dog, the asswipes over there were more than likely using as bait, and she'd told that dog she'd take care of him. That nothing would hurt him again and her mommy would fix him. So yeah, I'm angry. Angry that lowlife fuckers like them get to live…" I pointed to the two Widows, "…while those animals died for their entertainment and a few damn dollars."

"Not going to argue with you on that. I got two dogs and a cat at my house. Shit is sickening. But to answer your question on the dogfighting. What my officers got from them is the dog inside belongs to T-bone. He is a fighting dog, but the Widows aren't running a fighting ring. Seems T-bone has been participating in a few to showcase his dog. The dog has only fought a couple times, but he won his fights.

CM Books, LLC

"What you saw was the bait animals they've used the last couple weeks because Satan, the dog's name, has a fight or should I say did have a fight next week against another dog with no losses. They've been keeping him in shape, is the way they put it."

"Shut up, Satan! You're giving me a damn headache."

I heard my dad murmur 'fuck,' and I had to agree. But the one good thing out of it, the dog quieted.

We all walked through the back door, including the Chief, and in front of Satan's cage stood Freak. I wasn't surprised to see Freak there, but I was surprised the dog sat and listened. The dog was the typical breed of choice for dogfighting. The pit had a few battle scars, mainly around his head and face. He was all black and pure muscle. And I wasn't sure the thick chain and choker collar would hold him if he really wanted to break free.

I hadn't even realized that Freak had left the group outside and came into the building until I heard him yell at the dog.

"Got to admit when I heard him yell that I thought it was a joke until it suddenly got quiet."

"Prez, you know this isn't going to end well," Crank said.

"Come on, no one sees the humor in that statement coming from Freak. Truer words and all." Moose had lowered his voice before commenting, so Freak wouldn't hear him.

"Mark my words, we aren't getting out of here without that dog," Pinch griped.

CM Books, LLC

"Pinch might be right. I can guess why they call him Satan, but Beast would have been a better fit," I said as I looked over at Freak. He was squatted down in front of the cage talking to the dog while Shock stood off to the side.

"Well, all I'm saying is my ass is never going in the basement again," Tram said.

We'd all come back to the clubhouse for a well-deserved beer and had left the Chief and his men to their job.

When I got to the clubhouse, I'd called Raven and checked on Halo. He was going to be okay. They patched him up and he was resting. I didn't tell her everything that went down, but I did tell her the part about the fighting dog and that Halo was probably hurt being used as bait. Raven mentioned the stray Doc had patched up that ended up not making it, and we surmised it had more than likely been in same situation as Halo had been through. Instead of crying, Raven had gotten mad. By the end of the conversation with her, Reagan was finally getting her dog, and Halo would get a home.

I tipped my bottle of beer, drinking the last of it. I gave a chin lift to Latch when he handed me another.

"Prez, you have to tell us how you got the Chief to go along with it," Moose asked, and my dad smiled.

"I told him we had a vet in house that would make sure the dog had his shots and she'd evaluate him to make sure his rehabilitation was working. And I told him our local dog shelter didn't have the room, and that even if they did, they weren't equipped to deal with what the dog needed. And instead of putting the animal down, he should at least be given a chance to be rehabilitated. So he agreed we could take him."

I snorted. "Yeah, I'm sure you telling him that we were leaving, and good luck trying to get the dog out of that building even with animal control's help had nothing to do with his decision."

"It might have swayed him to our side a little more. Considering Freak was the only one it would let near him." Wild Bill grinned.

I held my beer bottle in the air. "And that's how Beast came to be a part of the Haven MC."

CM Books, LLC

Chapter Sixteen

Raven

Pulling up to the house and seeing Reed's bike already parked in the driveway gave me goosebumps in anticipation of what was to come. Exiting my car, I rushed to the door only to find it locked. With two kids and a job and temporarily living in my grandparents' house, Reed and I were having to get creative to enjoy some alone time, which made the appeal of his beautiful home our go-to place.

I fumbled with my keyring to find the key Reed had given me three weeks ago to the house. Once inside, I kicked the door closed and hurried down the hallway. As I reached Reed's opened bedroom door, I started toeing off my shoes only to come to a complete stop.

Reed sat naked with his back resting against the headboard, stroking himself. It was both beautiful and mesmerizing, and I was so captivated by the sight, I stood there speechless. I'd never get used to the sight of him and knowing he was mine.

"Did an appointment run over?" he asked, never faltering with his strokes, and the only ability I had was to nod. "Rav, if you don't stop staring at me like that. My plan to take my time with you is going to be over before it starts." Mesmerized, I watched his hand move up and down as he pumped.

I followed the motion of his hand a second more before I spoke, "There are no words for your body. It's like a temple." When I was able to pull my eyes away from his lap and back up to his face, he was smirking.

"If that's the case, I'm willing to let you pray over it. Why don't you strip those clothes off and come a little closer, babe." He patted the bed beside him. "I promise you won't be disappointed. Let me send you back to work with a smile on your face."

His words jarred me back and reminded me we were working with limited time. At breakneck speed, my clothes were off and laid haphazardly on the floor.

Reed chuckled. "That's the woman who was excited to get in here. Did you miss me?"

I moved toward the bed. "How do you know I was excited? For all you know, I could have been sitting in my car for ten minutes, debating if I'd rather eat lunch or see if you could satisfy my hunger."

"I've got enough to satisfy your hunger. And I watched you make your rapid approach because a few brothers came by this morning, and while they were here, they helped me install a few cameras around the property. Now come here and let me see how wet you are."

CM Books, LLC

Before I could answer, he reached out and pulled me to the bed and I was straddling his lap.

He placed a hand on each cheek, tilted my face up, and set his mouth on mine. Reed deepened the kiss, and it went from soft to demanding as he pushed his tongue in. Our tongues fought and our tastes combined as we explored each other's mouth. I melted into him. My chest pressed flush against his. And I felt his cock twitch between us as its hardness pressed against me.

When Reed broke the kiss, I was left breathless as he worked his way down my neck, kissing and nipping the skin as he found the tender spot between my neck and shoulder. His hands dropped to my shoulders and made their journey down my arms, leaving goosebumps in his touch's wake. His hands reached my waist and with a fluid motion, I laid on the bed on my back with him on top of me.

After a peck on the lips, Reed worked his way down my body, stopping first at my breasts. He moved between both, taking his time to worship each. A shiver went through me as his tongue circled, and then he sucked the peaked nipple into his mouth and bit gently. After moving to the other, giving it ample attention, he continued his journey down, stopping only briefly to circle his tongue around my belly button.

When his tongue swiped through my folds, and then the tip touched my swollen button, my back arched. He worked me until my center quivered and my body shook as my orgasm exploded.

CM Books, LLC

Reed kissed his way back up body and rested his weight on his forearms, his face hovering over mine.

"Damn, you are the most beautiful woman." With his eyes locked on me, my vision blurred with tears. He kissed away each one that escaped.

I'd never felt so worshipped in my life. Not even when he and I had sex in our youth. What a difference time and maturity made?

My heart beat for him as my body burned from the inside out. Staring into my eyes, he shifted and lined himself at my entrance. With the snap of his hips, he filled me. I gasped, my hands going to his back. The muscles underneath my hands bulged and strained as he began to move.

This time felt different than the others. His strokes were slow and easy but no less potent than our usual fast and furious due to time constraints.

Reed buried his face in my neck. "I want to continuing taking my time with you, but I'm struggling with my control. You feel too good."

"Then let go. I'll take you any way I can get you, Reed."

He pushed up, held his weight on one hand and grabbed one of my knees with the other, bending my leg and spreading me wide. His pace quickened, and I matched his thrusts. The burning from his previous slow movements intensified. The room filled with the sound of our labored breaths until my head bent back, my back arched, and I screamed his name as another orgasm ripped through me.

As I came down from my bliss, I couldn't believe the man hadn't gone over the edge with me, and I opened my eyes and looked at him. His focus was on where we were joined.

Reed lifted his eyes to mine. "I can't get enough of you." He pulled out, flipped me to my stomach, and slammed back in. The new angle had his balls hitting my clit each time he bottomed out.

The pounding he was giving me had yet another orgasm building. As he owned me body and soul, I closed my eyes and let him take me over the edge. How was it possible for this man to pull three orgasms from me? But the question in my head died as Reed draped his body over mine, and pounded into me until with one last thrust, he stilled, then spilled into me. He pulled out and our bodies collapsed on the bed. We laid quietly as we worked to get our breaths back.

With my eyes still closed, I felt the bed shift as he rose. Then I heard the sound of water running, then the warmth of a cloth as Reed wiped gently between my legs.

After taking the cloth back to the bathroom, he came back and slid into bed and pulled me into his arms. "I know you have to get back to work, but I'd give anything to lay in this bed with you for the rest of the day."

"Me, too. Sneaking around and stealing alone time as teenagers was fun and exciting. As adults, not so much." I reached up and rubbed the top of my head. "Especially when I still have a small knot on my head."

Reed moved my hand out of the way and felt the spot I was rubbing. "It's just a tiny one."

"Tiny? I saw stars."

"Babe, I'm the one who got injured. I've taken a fist to the face that didn't jar my teeth like your head did. First time I've been injured fucking in my truck."

I smacked arm. "It wasn't my fault. You're the one who couldn't wait and pulled off the road. We're lucky we didn't get caught, which, if I recall was why my head bumped into your chin in the first place."

I'd ridden into work with Gramps that morning and before closing, he was called to the shelter to have a look at one of the dogs that were sick. When he called and said he was going to be longer than planned and if I didn't want to wait on him at the clinic, then call to have Reed pick me up since he was coming to dinner.

"Hey, you're the one who panicked when you saw headlights and whacked my chin when you raised to get off me. And in my defense, I pulled off so I could get some lip time, other than a peck before we got to your grandparents' house. You're the one who climbed into my lap while we were kissing and started grinding on me."

"You should be a gentleman and take the blame."

"Oh, babe, I would…if I was a gentleman. Besides, we're not going to have to deal with it much longer. Come on, let's get dressed. I picked up a couple of subs on the way here. Didn't want you going back to work hungry. Though looking at the clock, you're going to be a little late anyway."

"I'd rather lay here with you than eat."

"Me, too, but I got something to show you after we finish eating."

"Okay, but it better be good." He swatted my butt, then roll out of bed. I stretched my deliciously sore muscles and then did the same.

After dressing then eating subs that we washed down with water, Reed led me upstairs.

"Oh, have you bought furniture for the other rooms?" I asked when he stopped us in front of a door to one of three empty bedrooms left empty upstairs. Ry's room was the only one furnished.

"Sorta," he said and opened the door.

"Oh my God, it's beautiful. When did you do all this?" I asked as I walked into the room. The walls were painted a soft pink with a purple border with every type of animal on it. A white princess bed sat against one wall with a canopy and a nightstand that sat beside it. There was a dresser with a mirror, a chest of drawers, a bookshelf with an attached desk, and a small rocker. Every piece matched down to the lamp that set on the nightstand.

On closer inspection, little things caught my attention. The frame on the table by the bed that held a picture of Reagan with her dad, Derek. The stuffed animals sitting in the rocker. Books in the bookshelf. Tears filled my eyes and I turned to look at Reed, who stood just inside the door watching me.

"Why did you do all this?"

"Well, a couple of reasons." He walked into the room and stopped in front of me, "I thought Reagan might like

215

having her own room here." He lifted his hand, and I gasped at the ring sitting in the middle of his palm. "I love you, Raven. I don't think I ever stopped. Will you marry me?"

The tears spilled over and ran down my cheeks. "Reed, I love you, too. And yes. Yes, I'll marry you."

He slid the ring on my finger and grabbed my hands. "You were mine the first time I saw you standing in front of that locker fighting the with the lock. And you'll be mine until I take my last breath. I had the room fixed for Reagan because I wanted to show her that she matters to me, not because of Ry or you. Because of who she is. And I want her to be happy. Hell, I want her to be mine. And I'm hoping you'll agree and consider letting me adopt her."

"You, Reed Borelli, are a good man. No wonder I love you."

"You make me better." He bent and pecked me on my lips. "Now, if you don't get out of here, you're going to be super late, and I don't want Doc getting mad and talking you out of marrying me."

"No way would he do that. He's always liked you. He was your biggest champion when it came to Ry. I want to blow off work and have you take me back to bed and celebrate, but the schedule for today is full. I can't do that to him."

"I know. So after work, I'll meet you at your grandparents' house, and we'll tell the kids together, then you guys can pack some things and move in here. After the kids go to bed, you and I will have our celebration. We can get married whenever you want, but I want you and the kids in this house."

"Alright, but may I suggest the kids stay with Gran and Gramps tonight so we can celebrate properly."

"That works for me. Now get out of here before I change my mind and carry you back to bed." Reed tugged and started leading me out of the room.

Once we were downstairs, he left me standing at the front door and told me not to move, then turned and walked down the hallway. When he came back with my keys, I frowned. "I could have gotten them."

"No, because I'm holding on by a thread and if you went in the bedroom, you wouldn't be getting out of the house."

"Does that mean I'm not getting a kiss goodbye? 'Cause that peck upstairs was not sufficient to seal a marriage deal." I grinned, and he glared, making me laugh.

Reed didn't answer, he opened the door and all but shoved me out of the house. I laughed all the way to the car where he unlocked it, opened the door and waited for me to get in.

Once I was in the car, he handed over the keys and waited until I was situated and had the car started. Then he started to push the door closed, but stopped halfway and leaned in.

"I'll give you a kiss worthy enough to seal the marriage deal tonight, and it won't just be one nor only on your mouth." He stood back up, shut the door the rest of the way and stepped back.

As I drove away, Reed was the one laughing while I glared.

CM Books, LLC

Chapter Seventeen

Keg

"I can't believe all that got done today," Raven said as we watched everyone drive away.

Raven and the kids had been in my house for two weeks, but we'd finally gotten all their stuff out of storage. She went through everything in storage she was keeping for the house and what they no longer needed—another trip to the dump for the prospects. At this point, I was just glad it was done.

"The club's a family, Rav. Everyone pitches in and does what they can for each other. You and the kids are part of that now." I pulled her to me and kissed the top of her head.

"Speaking of kids, I hope they made a dent in unpacking their stuff. At least that's what they're supposed to be doing upstairs." Raven started for the front door, and I followed.

"Ry was when I made the last trip upstairs to put a few boxes in the spare bedroom you designated for overflow until you could get to it. Reagan had her door closed, though, but I could hear her talking to Halo. I probably should have checked on her. Shit, it's going to take me a few to get used to this parenting stuff, I guess."

"You're doing an amazing job for being thrown into instant fatherhood. Besides, you will find Ry, even Reagan most of the time, are self-sufficient. Reagan still needs a little help with things, but other than that, you mainly just feed them and make sure they have clothes to wear."

"Kinda like Halo, minus the clothes."

Raven grinned. "I think the kids have some catching up to do with Halo. The dog might not wear clothes yet, but he has them beat in the behaving department, and he doesn't talk back."

"Let's hope he doesn't pick up the talking back."

"Bite your tongue. And as for clothes, Reagan already mentioned to me that she thinks he needs a coat since the weather is getting colder."

"If you get him a jacket at least make it leather. Maybe have some patches sewn on it. At least then maybe the guys won't laugh at him wearing clothes if it is something cool like a leather jacket."

Raven laughed as we walked into the living room. "It won't take long to finish in here," Raven said and approached the four various sized boxes stacked in the middle of the floor. "These boxes just have knickknacks and pictures for the walls."

220

"We can start in here if you want, babe." I pulled out the small knife I carried in my pocket and unfolded it, then sliced through the tape on the first box.

I hung the last picture on the wall an hour later. It wouldn't have taken that long if Raven hadn't changed her mind on which wall each picture looked best.

I walked into the kitchen to get a drink and looked around, not a box in sight. "Are there boxes hidden in the pantry or what?"

"Nope, thanks to Katie, Charlie, Macy, Tink, and Gran, everything was unpacked, washed and dried, then put away. Our bedroom is empty of boxes, too. While they helped Gran in the kitchen, I unpacked my stuff in there and put it all away. Pinch broke down the empty boxes and took them to the garage where the others are stacked."

I stood there and stared at the woman who'd been destined to be mine since the first time I saw her. I couldn't believe I'd never seen her around town before that day, or maybe I had and overlooked her. It didn't matter now just like the years apart didn't. I still nursed a little hurt over time lost with Ry, but he and I had made up ground in the two months since I'd found out he existed. But for the woman in front of me, her fate had been sealed the second she'd moved back. Raven was what made me want to live forever just to be able to wake up to her face every morning.

I sat the bottles of water I pulled out of the fridge on the counter and wrapped my arms around her when she walked in. Pulling her flush against me, I took her lips. She immediately opened for me, and I deepened the kiss.

221

"Oh, man. Gross, Dad."

I lifted my head, breaking our kiss and looked at Ry and Reagan as they stood in the doorway to the kitchen watching us.

"Get used to it, and I'll remind you about how gross you think kissing is when you start dating," Raven said and patted my chest and laughed.

I, on the other hand, couldn't find my voice. Raven squeezed my hand, and I looked down at her. She smiled. She realized it, too. It was the first time Ry had called me Dad.

"What are we having for dinner?" Ry asked and moved out of the way for the dog to pass. Evidently, the kid wasn't as affected by the monumental moment as I was.

Not wanting to make a big deal and embarrass myself or the kid, I swallowed the lump in my throat. "Depends on how much you and Reagan have left to do in your rooms."

"I'm done. I set the empty boxes outside my door," Ry answered and walked to the fridge and grabbed a drink.

"Okay. Well, I thought we could eat out to celebrate us all becoming a family."

"Can we go to the pizza place?" Ry asked.

Before I could answer him, Raven did. Probably because she knew I'd agree with him. "We are not going to eat pizza. We've had it twice this past week. We can go to the steak restaurant and eat like a normal family."

"Uh, Mom. Normally families eat at the pizza place."

I chuckled at Ry's comment. "He's got a point, Rav," I said and received an elbow in the side.

CM Books, LLC

Ignoring Ry and my shared fist bump, she turned to Reagan. "How about you, baby? Need some help with your stuff before we go out to eat?"

"Just the stuff you make me hang. I can't reach the bar in the closet." She walked past Raven and me where we stood at the counter, to the back door. "Come on, Halo," she said and opened the door and followed the dog out.

Raven stared at the closed door, then turned with a frown, and I asked, "What?"

She bit her lip like she always does when she's worried. "Not sure. Ry, did something happen upstairs?"

"No. She and Halo came out of her room at the same time I did. She seemed fine," Ry said as I watched him open and close cabinets. The one thing I found out about the kid when they moved in—he was a bottomless pit.

"Maybe she's tired, Rav."

"I don't think it's that. She gets cranky and whiny when she's tired. She seems upset."

"I'll go check on her," I said and walked out the back door.

I looked around, and at first I didn't see her. Then movement caught my attention. She was on the backside of the shed. As I grew closer, I noticed she had her head bent and was kicking her foot over the ground. I spotted Halo sniffing around just inside the tree line at the edge of my property. It had only taken the dog a week to learn the boundaries of the property. I didn't know how Reagan knew, but she'd been right about the dog needing her. He'd taken

223

to her right from the beginning, and wherever she was, he wasn't far away.

"You okay, Reagan?"

She raised her head, and I knew her mom was right when she looked up at me with those little brown eyes filled with sadness. I unconsciously rubbed by hand across my stomach. How men dealt with their little girls being upset was beyond me. No wonder Sami was always saying Ally had Speed and the other men at Black Hawk wrapped around her finger. 'Cause I would do anything to keep that look from ever entering Reagan's eyes.

"I guess."

"You sure? When I came out, you looked as though you were thinking hard on something. I don't ever want you to be scared to tell or ask me anything, Reagan."

"I'm sad."

Christ, two words from her that I could go the rest of my life not ever hearing. I was so out of my league. "What's got you sad?" I asked, and in my head, I silently added, *I'll kill or maim anyone, or do anything, to make it go away.*

"I can't go to the family dinner."

"Why not? Do you not feel good?"

"I'm not sick. It's 'cause I'm not part of your family."

"Of course you are, sweetheart." I had to ask, though fear gripped my heart with how she might answer. "Do you not want to be a part of my family?"

"Yes. But once you marry Mommy and adopt Ry, I'll be the only one with the last name Allen. So, I won't have any family anymore since my daddy is dead."

224

Damned if I didn't get another lump stuck in my throat. I dropped to my knees so I could be more at her level and cleared my throat, then prayed I didn't fuck this up. Kids needed to come with a manual.

"Well, I might just be able to fix that, but it will be up to you and your mommy."

"How?"

"I already talked with your mommy, and she's okay with it. We just hadn't talked with you yet. First though, a name doesn't make you family, sweetheart." I placed my big hand on her chest. "It's what in there that does. And in my heart, you are already part of my family. But I thought that since your daddy helped your mommy raise Ry. He loved and protected him and even shared his last name with Ry when I wasn't around. That maybe you'd let me do the same for you since your daddy's not here anymore. I already love you, Reagan. And I'll raise and protect you no matter what, but I sure would like to share my name with you, too. Would you let me adopt you?"

"My last name will be Borelli like yours, Mommy's and Ry's?"

"Yes."

"So I'll have two daddies like Ry, too?" With each question she threw at me, I felt the lump in my throat grow bigger.

"Yes."

"That means I can call you daddy, too?"

And that question did me in. I wasn't sure I could speak without my voice cracking, so I nodded. Then I gave up and let the tears fighting to be released go when Reagan lunged and wrapped her little arms around my neck and buried her face in my chest. I wrapped my arms around her while she cried.

Still holding her with one arm, I raised the other and used my hand to wipe at my own tears. I hadn't let tears fall since I was almost fifteen and my mom died.

When Halo ran past, I looked to see where he was going, and I saw Raven standing at the corner of the shed with her hands covering her mouth. She, too, had tears running down her cheeks.

I didn't know how long I knelt there and held Reagan before she quieted. I would have done it forever if she'd needed me to. But I knew that was unrealistic, and Ry proved it when he opened the back door.

"Hey! Are we going to eat soon or what? I'm hungry."

We had dinner as a family, then came home and worked more on getting things unpacked. Ry helped me break down the empty boxes while Raven helped her—our—daughter hang up her clothes. *Our* daughter. In that moment, I knew how my dad must have felt with Sami. I'd kill any man who broke her heart.

After the kids went to bed, I made a late call to the club's attorney explaining what I needed. Mr. Long's advice was that it would be easier for all involved to go through the adoption process the State of Washington required for Reagan's name change for Ry also. That way, Raven wouldn't have to explain why she'd allowed Derek to be

CM Books, LLC

added to Ry's birth certificate when he wasn't Ry's real father.

With Derek deceased, the process would be shortened because there was no other parent who had to sign away their rights. Only Raven's signature was required with the paperwork, then a home inspection followed by a court date so a judge could make it official.

I laid on my back in bed trying to catch my breath after showing Raven my appreciation for the family she'd given me. And turning the house into a home. "You know, I need to call Beth Evans and let her know she was right."

"First, who is Beth Evans?"

I chuckled at Raven's tone. "She is a sixty-plus-year-old married woman, and she was my realtor who found this house."

"Oh. Maybe I should call her and thank her for talking you into to buying it. It's amazing and beautiful."

"She didn't need to talk me into buying it, I loved the place when I saw it. It was big, but I didn't care. She told me to find a woman and fill the house with kids because that is how you turned a house into a home. Figured she get a kick out of knowing her words were true."

"Ah, I don't know her, but I like her."

"Something else I was thinking. I know we discussed having a cookout and having everyone over, but I want to hold off on it for a bit."

"Whenever you want to have it, it's fine with me."

"I want us to wait and get married after the court date is set for the kids. I thought since you wanted to skip having a wedding and wanted to just go to the courthouse, it shouldn't be a problem to get it done if not the same day, then close. You still sure you don't want a wedding, Raven?"

"I've had a wedding, Reed. Are you sure you don't want to have one?"

"I don't need a wedding, Rav. I only want the paper saying what I already know—you are mine. Just as the judge's signature on the kids' paper will show they are legally mine—my heart already knows that. It's for everyone else to know."

Raven raised up and planted a kiss on my chest. "You really are a good man."

I rolled until I laid on top of her. "Yeah, you won't think so in a minute. I've got my second wind."

I laid in bed thinking as I waited for sleep to take me as it had Raven. I knew at an early age that family didn't always mean just parents and kids, aunts, uncles, grandparents, and cousins. Family is anyone you love. Family wasn't just about the same blood running through your veins, it was about whether a person would stand behind or with you no matter what. It meant never having to face anything alone.

Family could be a mix-matched group of people who shared the same values. I always had my dad, my sister, and then my MC brothers. But it had taken Raven and the kids coming into my life to complete my family. I was glad I grabbed the second chance life offered me.

228

When my eyes closed and sleep was pulling me under, my thought was *no matter what the future held for me—with Raven and the kids by my side—I'll handle it.*

CM Books, LLC

CM Books, LLC

Epilogue

Crank

"Last year, did you ever picture any of us to be at this point?"

I chuckled as Reagan attempted to throw the rope for her dog, Halo, who jumped, missed and rolled, then I turned to Tram. "What? At a cookout?"

"Nah, three of us with ol' ladies. Come on, we've gone from club parties with drinking, women, and music to backyard barbequing. Don't it freak you out a bit?"

"We're drinking." I held up my beer. "There are women." I waved my arm at the group of women across the yard talking and laughing. "And music." I circled my finger in the air to signal the music softly playing from Keg's outdoor speakers around the pool.

Tram flipped me off, and I laughed. "You know what I mean. It's the atmosphere, drinking and gettin' rowdy, music blasting and women who are wearing less clothes and up for anything."

"Hey, I'm sure Keg would turn up the music. And while you're at it, ask the women if they'd take off a few items of clothing. I'm sure our brothers won't mind."

"You're hilarious, Crank. Just saying times are changing in the club."

"I see it as a good thing, Tram."

"Damn, our brother hasn't stopped smiling." Pinch sat down in the chair between Tram and me. I grinned at Tram, and he shook his head.

When I looked over at Keg, he was talking to Raven's grandfather with Raven tucked into this side. "Can't blame him. Good looking woman, two kids, a dog, and a home. Hell, brother is living the American dream."

"Hey, that's not everyone's dream." It seemed Tram wasn't going to give up on his aversion to family. He and I had similar backgrounds. I grew up in the system, and he might as well have because he'd had a mother who hadn't given two shits about him.

"I wouldn't mind it. Beats the hell out of growing old alone," I said and took a drink of my beer.

"Don't you like coming and going when you want, Crank? When you tie yourself to an ol' lady and family, your freedom goes out the window. Instead of jumping on your bike and taking off with your brothers whenever, you're at school functions, doctor's appointments, and spending your Saturdays mowing the lawn."

Pinch and I both turned our heads in Tram's direction. "What the hell, brother? You're in one helluva mood."

Tram shrugged his shoulder. "Just don't see why anyone would want to change their life to suit someone else. I watched my mom do it enough. She changed with every new guy she attached herself to until the last one finally broke her. Don't get me wrong, I'm happy for Keg, Moose, and Hawk. Even the others who've found a woman they're willing to give up their freedom for. Not for me, though. I enjoy being single."

"I think Moose, Hawk, and Keg would disagree with you about giving up anything for their women. And if you asked Smoke and Fire, I'm sure they'd agree with them. I'm not looking for a woman to make my ol' lady, but you bet your ass if I ever run into one that puts a smile on my face like those bastards, she's in my bed before she knows what hit her."

I followed where Pinch pointed using the beer bottle in his hand to see that Moose and Katie, along with Hawk and Charlie, were now standing with Keg and Raven. You only had to look at each brother's face to see they were content and loving life. Not that they were unhappy before—they'd just not known the pure contentment of having a woman brought them.

Thinking about women who had the ability to change a man, I thought of Mad. "Wasn't Madison coming with you today?"

Pinch's eyes narrowed on me. "She was on the schedule to close the bank. Why are you always worrying about my sister?"

233

I held my hands up in surrender. "Christ, I wouldn't have asked if I'd known you were going to snap my head off. I was at your house, asshole, when you told her Keg and Raven had extended the invite."

Keg had wanted to have everyone over for a cookout to celebrate Raven and the kids moving in with him. Then he decided to put off not only the cookout but marrying Raven until Ry and Reagan both were able to have his last name, too. It'd taken eight weeks to get everything officially done.

"Gee, Pinch, you do realize your sister is a grown ass woman who can make her own decisions. Even about who she dates or just wants to heat up the sheets with," Tram said, and Pinch raised from his seat.

I moved to put myself between him and Tram. "What is wrong with you, brother? I'm used to you on my case about your sister. Hell, all the brothers are used to you threating them about staying away from her. But you are wound up tight today."

"Come on, Pinch. I was just giving you a hard time. If you're going to act like this when I joke to get a rise out of you, what are you going to do to the unlucky bastard she brings home to meet you?" Tram said from his chair. He'd never stood, even with Pinch standing over him, ready to take him on.

I waited, interested in Pinch's answer, but he didn't say anything until after he plopped back into the chair. "I don't know. I think she's seeing someone now and is afraid to tell me. All I know is she's hiding something, and when I ask, she says she isn't. She flat ass lies and then turns it

CM Books, LLC

around on me. Saying shit like it's my fault she doesn't tell me anything and that I'm beyond protective and a control freak."

"Brother, I hate to say it, but you kinda are," I said and chuckled, hoping to lighten the mood.

"You think I don't know that. I finished raising her after our parents died. I don't know how to move from fill-in parent to brother. Every time I try to make the switch, telling myself she's an adult and I need to let her make her own choices, I think of some guy taking advantage of her, and I go bonkers. But what if she is hiding a boyfriend, what does that say about him? A chicken shit, I say if he can't deal with her brother."

I didn't answer him. I wasn't sure how. Luckily, the subject changed as our prez approached.

"How's it going, Prez?" I asked as he reached us.

"Couldn't be better." Prez looked over his shoulder at Keg, who now helped Ry push his dirt bike around the side of the house. Keg had bought it for an early thirteenth birthday present, and I thought the kid would sleep in the garage with it if Keg and Raven would let him.

"He getting the hang of the bike?" Tram asked, and Prez looked back at us with a grin.

"Oh yeah. Slow start, though. Boy had his momma about ready to disassemble the thing, and not in a good way. But once he got the hang of it, he took off. Damn, the kid is going to be hell on a motorcycle when he's old enough for one. Helped too that Keg lucked out with those woods behind his place. But Ry could use some new terrain to try out his skills."

"Well, the state has a ton of off-road bike tracks and trails. Different skill levels, too. You could take him to one of those," I suggested.

"Been looking into them. Thing is, I heard Ry mention to his mom that he wished he could go on a ride with us on his bike."

I groaned, knowing where this conversation was leading, and when I glanced over at Pinch and Tram, the resigned look on their faces said they knew, too. We'd all grown up around the area with the exception of Hawk. And at one time or another, we'd been to a trail or five.

"The one west of Vancouver rates high. Has eight miles of trail and I think a trail would be best for now. We can save taking to a track for later," Prez said, eyes twinkling because he knew the groaning and shit was for show. Big bad bikers and all. Why would we want to ride a trail on a dirt bike when we could ride our bikes all over the state and beyond? Because they were bikes and because they were built to take a better beating than our strictly for road bikes were was why.

"You trying to talk them into going on a trail ride with Ry?" Keg asked as he, Moose, and Hawk walked up. I could hear the motorbike and see Ry zipping through the woods.

"Shit, who needs talked into it. I'm game. Be fun, and Ry will get a kick out of it," Pinch said, and both Tram and I agreed.

CM Books, LLC

"I don't expect you boys to put money out buying a dirt bike, so I looked into renting some. There's a couple of places close that offer rentals. You boys want to go, I'll pick up the cost. Least I can do since it was my idea." Prez chuckled.

"When you want to do this? Winter's setting in and good days will be few until it starts moving out," Pinch said while he pulled his ringing cell from inside his vest.

"We can decide later. There's no rush, Ry will just be thrilled you guys are on board," Keg said, then chuckled. "Maybe it will settle him down. He's driving Raven nuts with all the motorcycle talk, and if that isn't bad enough, he told her last week, he was prospecting when he turned eighteen. Thought I saw a couple of her hairs turn gray on that one."

"Well, at least you know Raven won't go on the trail ride. Charlie's going to get pissed when I tell her she can't come. I know her ass will want to go even if none of the other women do," Hawk chimed in, and we all laughed.

"Madison? You there, Madison?" Pinch's words and tone had everyone going quiet and turning in his direction.

"What's going on, Pinch?" I asked.

"I'm not sure," he said as he looked at us, then took the phone from his ear and tapped a button on the screen. Muffled voices could be heard through the speaker, but the words couldn't be made out.

"What the hell did Madison do, butt dial you?"

Before Pinch could answer, a man's voice came out of the phone, "Bitch, I told everyone to turn over their phones!"

The next thing we heard was Madison scream followed by the distinct sound of a gunshot, then nothing but silence as the line went dead.

CM Books, LLC

Acknowledgments

To everyone who waited patiently for Keg's book – thank you. I hope his story was worth the wait.

And, a special thanks to Paul, from Photography by Paul Henry Serres, and cover model, Mikaël Jodoin, for the perfect photo for Keg's cover.

Carson

CM Books, LLC

About the Author

Carson Mackenzie enjoys writing romance with a real feel inside the stories. She writes with the belief not every man is a jerk and not every woman needs saving.

Carson lives in the South with one of her sons, a Great Dane and two adopted shelter dogs that keep the household in line. Books have always been a part of her life. There is nothing better to her than curling up and relaxing with a good story and losing herself in someone else's world for a few hours.

Writing stories and growing as an author with each book is her goal. She wants to reach the level where a reader knows when they see her name, they can trust in the fact there will be a good story as they flip through the pages.

Carson's been her writing journey for a few years. As she's finally starting to settle in, her only regret is she hadn't started sooner.

Stay up to date with what I'm working on:

Webpage: www.carsonmackenzieauthor.com/
Goodreads: www.goodreads.com/author/show/14764937.Carson_Mackenzie

CM Books, LLC

CM Books, LLC

Books by Carson Mackenzie

Black Hawk MC

Speed
Crusher
Devil
Ghost
Jag
Coast
Flirt

Haven MC

Moose's Regret
Hawk's Bounty
Keg's Revelation

Desert Phoenix MC

Desert Phoenix Rising

CM Books, LLC

Standalones
Her Way or No Way
Two Paths One Destiny

CM Books, LLC

CM Books, LLC

www.ingramcontent.com/pod-product-compliance
Lightning Source LLC
Chambersburg PA
CBHW022112240626
47153CB00007B/2330